NUTS IN MARCH

Robert Metcalf

Dedication

To Victoria. For your patience. And for being there. Always.

Contents

Prologue

Albert had just finished eating his best friend. Licking his lips with his forked tongue, he decided that the dog was next on the menu, beginning with what he considered the most tender and delicious segment: a leg. But, no matter how many of the canine's limbs Albert consumed – or which corner he chose – by the time the appendage had been devoured the canine still had a complete set, even enquiring if Albert would like a little salt to sprinkle on the half-devoured thigh. Normally, he would have told the dog to go stick its head up its own backside, but having just bitten off a lump of fur made speech impossible. And anyway, he had been taught his manners at a very early age and knew that talking with his mouth full was not acceptable.

Albert is a vegetarian adder (except for the odd accident) and is having a nightmare! Eating the tortoise, his best friend, first, followed by the dog. Even the frog isn't safe.

Suddenly, a faraway voice interrupted his canine feast. It was Granny Anna…

Chapter 1

Anna the Anaconda was contemplating making a break for it, going on the run, or, in her case, on the slither. She and all her friends in the snake house had, on and off, discussed breaking out. But no one had been given the opportunity. Until now. Fate had suddenly given her a chance to be free; free to move on from working in the travelling zoo and the most boring job in the world. She and all the other inmates, her friends, including boa constrictors, rattlesnakes and various other deadly reptiles, had to perform from behind reinforced safety glass. Well, it should have been safety glass, and it had been until some silly bugger dropped it. Money being scarce, the zoo had to come up with a cheaper way to separate the dangerous reptiles from the paying customers. Now, thanks to the zoo manager, the barrier separating spectators from some of the most poisonous snakes in the world was a sheet of 'Extra Strength' easy clean cling film. The paying public, knowing nothing of the danger they were in, continued to file past, pointing and laughing at the stupid performing snakes.

Anna and her friends, of course, weren't as daft as the punters believed them to be and knew they could quite easily have broken through the cling film at any time. But, after discussing the situation, they all decided – for now – to play dumb. And anyway, they just couldn't be bothered, and voted to do nothing about it; well, almost nothing. Every now and then, Anna and her friends, just to relieve the boredom, would pretend to be stuffed, remaining completely rigid for hours on end. One or two even lay on their backs, tails in the air, forked tongues hanging out, trying their hardest not to laugh at the angry customers, all of whom demanded their money back. Eventually, the snake-handlers worked out what was happening, and, after a few gentle prods with long sticks and bribing them all with promises of a few extra dead rodents, Anna and her friend went back to pretending to be mean and nasty. But, to be perfectly honest, their hearts weren't really in it.

On occasions, the zoo was inspected by an officer from the RSPCA; the inspection lasting for no more than an hour or so, followed by a nice cup of tea, a couple of bourbons for the officer and a chat with the ticket collector's pretty daughter. On one inspection, however, the RSPCA had the temerity to send a hard-faced trainee, and he was determined to upset everyone – animals as well as staff – and show them how keen he was. Surprising everyone, including the trainee, the inspection went well. That was, until he got to the snake compound. It was explained to him by the grinning snake-handler that it was best not to get bitten by any of the reptiles. Unfortunately for the zoo, after that off-the-cuff remark, the young trainee got the hump, and was now on the warpath. Happening to pass the rattlesnake enclosure, he espied one of the snakes, Marge, was missing her trademark rattle. It was explained patiently to him that the unfortunate reptile had happened to be too close to a sliver of glass when it was accidentally dropped on her tail (it was thought best not to tell him where the glass originated from). The snake-handler explained to the young inspector the loss of her rattle wasn't at all life-threatening and Marge didn't seem to mind anyway

How it happened, why it happened, or when it happened, didn't matter to the young lad. He insisted that the horny rim be reattached by the time he returned in the morning to finish his inspection, or else he would not sign the safety certificate. And everyone in the zoo knew what that meant. With that, the young lad was off. Teach them to laugh at me!

The manager of the travelling menagerie, far cleverer than some stuck up his own bum oik, immediately sent one of his assistants into town to buy a rattle from the local toy shop, and to then attach the toy to the tail end of the reptile.

As promised, at eight o'clock on the dot, the young officer, complete with clipboard and his favourite bright red pen, returned to complete his task. Directed immediately to the rattlesnake's sleeping quarters, it was explained to him that the reptile had yet to wake and have its breakfast, but, if he so wished, he could try to coax her out himself. This time, the snake-handler, ever so conveniently, forgot to mention anything about being careful. If the stroppy git was bitten, tough!

Not as stupid as he looked, there was no way the inspector was going to stick his head inside the nest, deciding that it would be a lot safer just to give the receptacle a kick. Nothing happened for about thirty seconds; then the sound of someone

– or something – yawning, immediately followed by a very satisfactory and perfectly toned rattle. With a rather smug look on his face, job seemingly done, the inspector was about to exit the compound when he was amazed to hear a very tuneful rendition of a nursery rhyme, coming from inside the rattlesnake's den: 'The wheels on the bus go round and round'. What the hell was that? A musical snake? No. It can't be! Unable to believe his ears, he, ever so foolishly, gave the nest another, even harder, punt.

Inside her den, Marge, abruptly awoken from her dream, wondered what all the noise was about, and where the music was coming from. Annoyed at being awoken at this time in the morning (it was her day off, and she had been promised she could have a lie-in), she stuck her head out of the nest. Normally a very kind and placid rattlesnake, Marge saw who had been responsible for waking her up, lost her temper and decided that the noisy so-and-so needed to be taught a lesson and proceeded to chase the lad around the enclosure. Off he ran, followed closely by a, seemingly, very angry snake, who was followed even more closely by the song, 'This old man, he played one, he played knick-knack…'

The remainder of the tune was lost when the inspector – eventually – managed to get to the exit and the door was slammed shut. What he wasn't to know was that Marge was just as confused as the poor boy, and believed it was she who was being pursued. As fast as she had been, there was no getting away from the insane music, which, to her, seemed to be coming out of her bum.

Heart thumping, a look of horror on his face, and still in shock, the young inspector was convinced that he could hear the snake banging on the door to get out and, he thought, to get at him. Again he heard the snake's rattle, followed, this time by a new rhyme, 'Humpty Dumpty sat on a waalll...'

That was it! He was out of here, not even stopping to sign the safety certificate. Calling over his shoulder, he informed the manager that everything was satisfactory and that he would post it on.

The assistant manager, when asked about the musical rattle, pleaded his innocence, explaining that it was the only one in the shop. No one believed a word of it. The smirk the assistant had on his face all day didn't help either. The only downside to the joke was that the manager insisted that his assistant paid for new batteries for the rattle out of his own pocket.

*　　*　　*

With another season over, the keepers began readying themselves for the next move, first making sure that all the animals were safe and comfortable, then striking the tents and dismantling the solid structures as quickly as possible and down to the local café for pie and chips before the long journey.

Unfortunately, in the rush to complete their tasks, Anna's cage had, inadvertently, been left open.

Chapter 2

Anna was having second thoughts. Should she take a chance, or should she bottle it? Her friends in the snake house, though, were all for it. in fact, her best friend, Bob the Boa, insisted she should, "Go now." Otherwise the opportunity would be lost, and she would forever regret it. Someone, forked tongue firmly in cheek, began to make clucking noises. That was it. The one thing she wasn't was chicken. With a final sad look over her shoulder, she slipped out of her cage and disappeared into the overlong grass.

No one missed Anna, and it wasn't until the travelling zoo reached their next venue, almost two hundred miles away, that anyone noticed she was gone. Much too late to send anyone back to look for her, the staff had to try and persuade one of the young boa constrictors to deputise for her. It was Bob who eventually volunteered. It had after all been the boa who had prompted Anna to go in the first place. He would have to be painted of course (the colours on both snakes differed completely). First, though, a promise to use only washable emulsion paint, and being fed extra mice on Sundays. Both parties finally agreed and were happy with the arrangements. Sensibly, not wishing to be caught out again, the manager did the shopping for the paint himself.

Although now alone, Anna had picked the perfect place in which to desert. Close to the zoo's temporary site was a large meadow with a river close by, and there would, of course, be numerous boggy patches for her to wash herself in and keep clean. Also, Albert – who she will meet very shortly – would help her to adjust to her different environment. He would also help her to get over the loneliness she was bound to feel whenever she thought of her friends, all those miles away. Although she didn't know it yet, she had just over an acre of overgrown wasteland in which to roam around. First, a quick recce of the area, and then, hopefully, a meal and, more importantly, finding somewhere to stay. Still not yet fully grown, her appetite would not be a bother to her. It would be to any unwary foxes or badgers, but not to her. Not yet, anyway. Her future surrogate grandson, Albert, would, coincidentally, be one of the first creatures she would happen upon.

On her first recce, Anna spotted who she thought were four friends: two foxes and two distant cousins of hers, adders, seemingly playing a game of 'catch me if you can'. So, for the moment, she decided to stay hidden and enjoy watching, before showing herself and saying hello. She smiled, remembering the fun and games she and all her friends used to have at the zoo; not too unlike what she thought the four pals were doing now.

The pair of foxes, a dog fox and a vixen, were not playing games. In fact, what was about to happen would send Anna into a rage. The male fox and the vixen were about to dispatch both adders; the female cornering the younger snake, while the male, snarling viciously, readied itself to pounce on the younger snake's brave, elder companion. The fox was first into the attack, feigning to go right, then snapping with deadly intent. But the female snake was on to his game and was just that little bit quicker, sliding to her left, circling him, ready to strike at the first opportunity. Never taking her eyes from him, the female snake attacked, striking at the fox's unprotected rump. He seemed to know exactly what she was planning and leapt backwards, then, in an instant, he was on her. Almost quicker than the eye could see, he pounced, sinking his teeth into her unprotected neck, swiftly shaking the life out of her.

It was then that Anna lost her temper and changed everything. Both foxes had, incidentally, started the day as the diners, but, very rapidly, the dog fox became the dinner. The vixen, having just seen her soon-to-be-ex-partner almost disappear down the monster's throat, believed that now was as good a time as any to bugger off and leave the pair of them to it. Still, you couldn't blame her.

Anna, having just dispatched one of Albert's assailants, introduced herself to the young snake.

Chapter 3

Albert was the eldest of three brothers and two sisters – to a single mum – all of whom lived with their elderly grandad. It was no great surprise to his mother that Albert was a vegetarian. It wasn't by choice either. His grandfather was vegetarian, and his grandfather before him. Strange as it seems for an adder, every first-born male in Albert's family never ate meat. Although, in his case, and no one could ever work out why, whenever the opportunity came along, he ate millipedes. He didn't want to, but sometimes he just couldn't help himself. In fact, any insect unlucky enough to have more than a couple of dozen legs is fair game to Albert. Apparently, his mother had explained, this was a seeming hiccup in his complicated DNA.

Life in the nest was difficult for Albert, not because he was unhappy with family life but because of the arguments he used to have with his siblings, who thought nothing of bringing home half-digested rodents just to tease him with and wind him up. Luckily for him, his brothers and sisters soon left the nest and he was able to get on with eating his vegetables in peace.

When he was old enough and, with his curiosity eventually getting the better of him, he asked his grandad why he was a vegetarian, and why was it always the firstborn.

Albert senior was never the most sociable of adders. In fact, he was, and always had been, a right miserable so-and-so, who was forever upsetting everyone with his constant complaints. Reluctantly and grudgingly, he ordered Albert to slide on to his lap. Still grumbling darkly, he closed his eyes for a moment, Albert junior assumed a position, in concentration. He waited... and waited. About to ask again, he heard his grandad snoring. The grumpy old sod had fallen asleep! Not wishing to disturb the old snake, he slipped quietly away.

Unseen by his young grandson, the ancient snake opened one eye and giggled. Rather than embarrass himself, he had feigned sleep. To be honest, he didn't have the first clue why Albert – or anyone else for that matter – was vegetarian. No matter how many times Albert tried, he never got a sensible answer from his grandad, so in the end he stopped asking.

A miserable old sod he may well have been; nevertheless, he was far from being stupid. Knowing that his time was almost up, he relented. Having mercilessly teased his grandson for what now seemed a very long time, the least he could do for the younger snake was to pass on the facts of an adder's life to him. He called Albert to his side.

"Closer," he was ordered.

At last, the old snake was going to explain why he was a vegetarian, albeit in Albert's case with a bit of a hiccup now and then.

The old snake chuckled to himself.

"Albert," his grandad began.

The young snake held his breath and waited.

"Always remember, if you ever want to get your own back, make sure you pee directly into the wind."

The old snake laughed out loud at the disappointed look on Albert's face.

"Sorry, son. Only kidding. Seriously, though, what I am about to tell you is very, very important. Something that was passed down to me by my grandad and his grandad before him and will help you for the rest of your life. Understood?"

Albert replied that yes, grandad, he understood.

"And it was drummed into me again and again that a grandad should never, ever, forget to pass on the secrets of an adder's life, so when the time comes for you to mate with your girlfriend, you will get it right."

Albert frowned.

"Go courting. Procreate, son. Understand?"

Albert said he did, although, to be honest, he hadn't a clue what his grandad was on about.

"Good," his grandad continued, "because, what I have to say will probably come as a bit of a shock to you. Now, listen very carefully. We adders possess more than one, er…"

Albert waited.

"Remember, adders have…have…two, erm… It's imperative you never, ever forget we vipers have always had…two…two…"

Exasperated that he couldn't remember, he tried once more; this time, sadly, for the last time.

"Son, never forget you have…have… Wait! I'll get it in a minute. Never, forget…! Damn Albert, what the hell was it I was supposed to remember?"

With that last attempt, the old snake sadly expired.

Believing that his grandad was feigning sleep again, Albert patiently waited. He still didn't trust the old bugger not to open his eyes and start giggling again. He had been fooled too many times to take any chances. Sadly, after waiting a few minutes, he had to admit even his grandad couldn't hold his breath that long. He slid into the kitchen to inform his mum.

Although any death in a family is a traumatic experience, and, although the old snake was one miserable fart, forever making everyone's life a misery, the grieving process was no less traumatic for Albert and his mother. Unfortunately, grieving in the wild for long wasn't possible. It was Mother Nature's hard and fast rules that had to be adhered to. This meant that Albert and his mum had to leave the den immediately; the last of his siblings having left some time ago. It wouldn't be very long before the local predators realised there was an easy meal going free, so staying wasn't an option.

After saying their goodbyes, the pair sadly slid quickly away and began the search for new accommodation. Soon enough, they arrived at what they thought to be the ideal lodgings: a large hollowed-out tree trunk with plenty of spare rooms. After a closer recce, to make sure no predators lay in wait, they declared that this was now their new home. Being a mother and very domesticated, Albert's mum soon had it shipshape.

*　　*　　*

The following morning, Albert and his mother set out in search of food. However, the pair were being watched and hadn't got very far when they were confronted by two hungry foxes: a dog fox and a vixen. Unable to escape the trap the pair had set for them both, Albert and his mother would have to do their best and try and defend themselves. It wouldn't be easy. Separating him from his mother, the female fox cornered Albert, while the male set about attacking his mum.

The dog fox, sharp snout snapping viciously at his mother, began his assault. There was nothing Albert could do to help either. Each time he attempted to get close enough to aid his mother, the vixen snapped at him and he was forced to retreat. Horrified and helpless, he could only look on.

His mother, weaker now, was no longer able to defend herself. Her only chance would be to feign death and hope to catch the fox off guard; at the very least allowing her to slide into the thick undergrowth, giving her a slim chance to get her breath back. The fox, a mature adult, was not to be fooled. Pouncing on the exhausted reptile, sinking his teeth into her neck, he shook the life out of her.

Now it was Albert's turn.

First his grandad, now his mother. Albert was in a state of shock. Nevertheless, he had no other option but to try to defend himself. Dwelling on the loss of his mother was not an option; he had to protect himself. He was sensible enough to realise that there could only be one outcome to this uneven contest but he would do his best and was determined to go down fighting. Instinctively, he poked out his tongue. Amazingly, both foxes reared back in horror; the vixen already disappearing into the dense undergrowth, the male frozen to the spot. Blimey, Albert thought, perhaps now would be as good a time as any to be somewhere else.

Before he could move, however, sliding out from the undergrowth, a monster appeared, rapidly advancing towards the petrified fox. A split second later, whatever it was had his mother's killer firmly and unmoving in its massive jaws. Albert believed it was to be his turn next, and who could have blamed him? The Loch Ness monster was alive and well and on holiday! There would be no getting away from this one!

To his utter relief and amazement, however, instead of swallowing him whole the giant gave him a huge grin.

"Know anywhere to stay around here?" the colossus enquired, cheerfully.

Yes, of course he did. (Well, he wasn't about to say he didn't, was he? Not to something as big as this, whatever the hell it was.) What's more, she could have the biggest bedroom. Of course, he was upset at the shocking way his mother had died, and he of course cared, but death was such a matter of fact in the world Albert lived in. It could well have been him the foxes had chosen first. And there was nothing to say it wouldn't be his turn next. Although, with this monolith on his side, who's to say he couldn't rule the world? Having taken Anna to the den and shown her around, he explained to her that it was his mother who had been killed by the fox.

Full of sympathy for him – he was obviously hurting – she insisted he get his head down for a rest. It was almost the end of October anyway, so it was time he curled up and slept. She would look after him while he was in hibernation and would wake him when it got a little bit warmer. She would get her own head down later when he had settled down properly and gone into a deep sleep.

Albert yawned. She was right. He was knackered. Before bedding down for the winter, however, he thanked her for being such a kind and caring snake.

"Thank you, Granny Anna, for saving me."

Anna was almost in tears. For the first time in her life, she had done something worthwhile. She sighed, watched as Albert curled up and went to sleep, then silently slithered away. It was about time the dead fox was given a good send-off. She also needed to check out her new neighbourhood, and meet a few of Albert's friends.

Having promised Albert not to hunt in his meadow – at least until he had introduced her to all his friends anyway – she did have a quick look around but found nothing of interest, so she quickly returned to the den and checked that Albert was safely tucked up and asleep, before getting her own head down.

It had been a long and traumatic day for the two of them.

Chapter 4

Five months on, spring has arrived, and Speedy the Tortoise, Albert's best friend, is in trouble. His problem: he is an inveterate gambler and just can't stop. To be fair, he has tried his hardest to stop, even – once – joining the local gamblers help group 'All Bets Are Off', and, of course, it had been a disaster. At his first appointment, while he was in the waiting room, he just couldn't help himself and lost ten pounds, to a magpie. The second appointment was twice as costly, losing twenty quid to – of all people – the help group's counsellor. He considered that it would be less hassle and costly if he just gave in and carried on gambling his life away. Which is why he now finds himself outside Billy's betting shop, as usual, on the wrong end of a losing streak.

"Ow! You've nearly broken my tail!" Speedy complained.

This wasn't very surprising, seeing as he had just been booted out of the bookmaker's betting shop. Again. He had been followed outside by the bookmaker's henchman: the thug who had unceremoniously booted him up the bum.

"It will be more than your backside that's broke," he warned, "if you don't pay us back what you owe! Now, bugger off!"

"I'll get you all back, you flat-faced git!" Speedy retorted, albeit to himself. Then, taking a deep breath, bum still hurting, he limped back into the betting shop and demanded to be allowed to speak to the bouncer's boss, Billy. "I have a proposition he may be interested in," he explained.

Expecting another kick up the arse, he tucked his tail back into his shell. Surprisingly, he was granted five minutes. It was, Speedy thought, about time he turned the tables on Billy the Bookmaker. Give him a taste of his own medicine. Ushered into the office, he was told by Billy to get on with it. Nervously, he explained his proposition.

"You have a race meeting soon, right?"

The bookmaker's cold eyes stared coldly into his. Speedy took that to mean he could continue.

"Would you be interested in an offer of mine?"

Billy nodded for him to carry on.

"At the meeting, I will race against your favourite hare."

The bookmaker's sidekick growled bad temperedly and picked him up by the scruff of his neck, ready to turf him out once again.

The bookmaker intervened. "Let him finish. Then you can boot him out. Continue."

Speedy hurried on.

"Right. Let me explain. My idea is this: myself and your hare, Jill, would pretend to race against each other, like those silly clown contests they have at the circuses. A joke race. And, because hibernation is almost over, you are going to get a lot of bored spectators turning up, if only for a bit of fun and, of course, they will all be putting on small bets. And a lot more creatures will want to come, if only for a laugh, and that will mean lots more paying customers. What do you think?"

Nothing happened for a few seconds. And Speedy hadn't yet got his promised good hiding. A good sign?

Ever the businessman, the bookmaker wanted to know what Speedy got out of it. Speedy explained what was in it for him. "Let me off my latest debts and let me come back into the betting shop."

Much to his surprise, Billy liked the idea and ordered him to elaborate. He explained that the dash – it couldn't really be called a race – between himself, Speedy, and one of the swiftest creatures on the planet, capable of reaching an astonishing fifty miles an hour, would be over fifty yards, with the tortoise given a forty-yard start. That way, Speedy explained, the crowd would, if only for a short period, pee themselves laughing, watching a slow-moving tortoise pretending to be an Olympic sprint champion. Not only that, after the race, they would all, very likely, stay for the rest of the day, losing even more money.

After giving it some thought, Billy liked the idea and was happy to go along with it. If, and only if, the day was successful, would Billy then wipe Speedy's betting debts off the books.

* * *

Many years ago – forgotten by almost everyone – there was the ancient so-called 'fable', when a tortoise and hare had first raced one another. And, as it happens, by a lucky coincidence the triumphant tortoise in question just happened to be an ancestor of Speedy. What went on and how it had all happened all those years ago has been a closely guarded secret, passed down from family member to family member, and was only ever to be used in an emergency. This present situation he had got himself into, was, as far as he was concerned, such a crisis. What Billy and all his staff weren't to know was that Speedy and Jill, the hare he was to race against, had become acquaintances, having shared the odd carrot together sometimes. So, first thing in the morning, he went to see Jill, to say hello. Her form wasn't far away from his home, so it didn't take him long to get there. And, by the look of her – as usual, fur dishevelled, ears floppier than usual, uncombed fur – she had only just this minute woken up. Speedy immediately put his plan into action, explaining to the half-asleep hare that he had brought her breakfast and, knowing Jill's liking for mushrooms, he just happened to have a small bagful of the delicious fungi. Thanking him, she wolfed down the lot in double-quick time.

As part of his plan, Speedy did this each morning, including on the day of the race. However, on the morning of the race, he changed her favourite tipple, the puffball, to the more potent stinkhorn, explaining to Jill that, unfortunately, he hadn't had his delivery of the puffball yet. But, as he explained to her, the stinkhorn was just as nice. But, as everyone in the tortoise family was aware, unless the fungi are in the egg stage, this is a no, no. He, of course, along with members of his family, knew that even the smallest morsel of the fully-grown fungi would soon make the recipient very sleepy. Nothing sneaky. Just a little help for any tortoise with a touch of insomnia. Usually.

Bidding the soon-to-be giddy girl a good morning, he went off to update his brothers, sisters and every other relative he could find who was in on the scam. And yes, they had all clubbed all their resources together, collected as much money as they could and had placed their bets on him. So, it was now up to him to do the business.

Billy the Bookmaker had done himself proud and the field he used for his races was packed with curious spectators. Because, as Speedy had explained, it was the final days of hibernation, a lot of early risers had turned out and creatures of all types were there. Rabbits sat alongside hares, voles and field mice sat next to each other; even those snotty-nosed, stuck up their own behinds red squirrels were there, chatting with almost everyone. Although, like everyone else, they drew the line when it came to those rough, ever-so-common common shrews.

All of the dedicated gamblers had made the effort to be there for the serious races. Though most spectators were only there to see Speedy. A tortoise racing against a hare? Goodness, whatever next! Sworn enemies had declared a truce, but, once the race was over and the field had emptied, it was once again every poor sod for itself.

Surprising everyone, the first of the competitors to arrive was Speedy; greeting his relatives, telling a few one-liners (he was a born joker). To add a little fun, one of his relatives had painted a white go-faster stripe across his shell. He was soon spotted by the crowd. Immediately, he was whoop, whooped by everyone, with lots of encouraging cheers from his family members.

Speedy was full of himself. "Thank you, thank you…" he began, before getting the nastiest of looks from Billy; shutting him up. Ten minutes later, he arrived at his start line, ready for the off. Of Jill, there was still no sign. Getting restless, the crowd began to boo and jeer, shouting good-naturedly at the bookmaker, "Fiddle!" "We want Jill!" "We want Jill!" "Boo!" "Boo!"

Billy was about to lose his temper. Luckily, for all concerned, Jill arrived, quieting the crowd. Helped to the start line by her puzzled friends, a very tired looking hare was still contemplating whether or not she should have stayed in bed. Startled by the sudden cheering of the crowd, she turned to flee, tripped and fell flat on her face. The crowd roared with laughter, cheering her every time she tried and failed in her attempt to get to her feet. Eventually, her friends, with a little help from Billy's minders, managed to keep her upright long enough for the off.

Earlier than scheduled, the starter's pistol cracked, "BAAANG," catching everyone by surprise, including the starter: a badger. Not used to handling anything more lethal than an earthworm, he had accidentally got his claws caught in the safety guard, pulling the trigger by accident; the discharge setting fire to his fur. A few spectators, assuming something more sinister was happening, panicked and headed for the exits. Others roared with laughter; everyone assuming that Billy had deliberately put on this brilliant sideshow for their benefit.

Meanwhile, the poor badger was still rolling around on the ground, attempting to extinguish his blazing fur.

Speedy, not too sure what was going on, ducked back into his shell, saving himself from the mini-stampede. However, an earthworm, minding its own business, and having only just wriggled its way out of the cold ground, was squirming across the earth to the still burning badger with the sole purpose of warming itself up. Not quite alert enough to get himself out of the way, he was lucky not to be completely flattened. He was the sole casualty. Wriggling madly, stunned but otherwise intact and unharmed, the invertebrate was immediately, and reluctantly, put on a stretcher and taken to the casualty tent to be examined by the volunteer nurses: robin redbreasts. The ungrateful patient, insisting that there was nothing wrong with him, pleaded could he please go now? but the nurses, who up until now had had no patients, were bored beyond belief, and very, very annoyed that no one had the decency to die on them. At last, they had a genuine patient. Perhaps this one would have the good grace to be their first fatality. With that in mind, they were not going to let him get away so easily.

Obviously not as busy as they would like to have been, the robins insisted that the unwilling invalid stay and be nursed, have a cup of tea, shut up, stop complaining and lie still. To be certain that the noisy worm wasn't just being brave, he was carried to the examination room. Disappointingly, it was confirmed that the only anomaly the worm was suffering from was an over-active mouth. No matter which way the caring robin redbreast volunteer nurses looked at it, it was obvious that the patient wasn't anywhere near – voluntarily – to popping his clogs. So, because of the racket he had been making, upsetting other patients (well, he would have if there had been any), he could now, sadly, be discharged. Unfortunately for the worm, after giving the nurses unprovoked and unwarranted verbal abuse, he, unsurprisingly, took a turn for the worst and was very quickly put out of his misery, and laid to rest. So, the robin redbreast nurses, in the end, got their cadaver. (And delicious he was too.)

*   *   *

It was Billy's minders who restored order and who had managed to persuade the rioters to return. Five minutes later, the unruly spectators were seated, and proceedings could again begin.

"CRAACK!"

This time, the badger, eyes tightly shut, fur still smouldering, got it right, and everything went to plan. Jill, to the good-natured boos of the crowd, set off at a tremendous pace, and ten wobbly seconds later she hurtled past Speedy as if the tortoise was standing still, which, in fact, he was. Then, this time, to the cheers of the crowd, Jill turned around and sprinted just as swiftly past the point where she had been, seconds ago. Luckily, her friends rugby-tackled her to the ground before she disappeared into the distance. The crowd were in raptures, whoop, whooping once again.

With the utmost difficulty, her pals managed to get Jill facing the right way, and she was off again. But, after her first surge, it just didn't happen for her. Staggering forwards a few yards, sideways a couple of feet, forwards again, before, to the delight of the ecstatic crowd, once again falling flat on her face, this time snoring loudly. No amount of prodding and poking by her friends made any difference. She was out for the count. The crowd, mesmerised by the doe's antics, began clapping and cheering her. She was great fun. A real star.

While all this has been going on, Speedy slowly, ever so boringly slowly, had been puffing his way to the finish line. A shrill blast on a whistle indicated to everyone that the race was over. Speedy had won. Once again, a tortoise had triumphed in a run-off, against a champion hare.

The crowd, hearing the final whistle, began cheering again, everyone chanting, "Speedy! Speedy!" The triumphant tortoise waved, basking in the glory.

*   *   *

At the end of the day, all the creatures went home happy, Speedy's family went home a few quid richer and even animals who didn't normally bet won a few quid on him. Everyone was satisfied with the day's entertainment. That is, everyone with the exception of an angry bookmaker, had had a grand day out. An exorbitant amount of money had been put on the tortoise to win, and Billy was furious, convinced, no, certain, he had somehow been cheated. But, rather than lose face in front of all the punters, he had given everyone what was owed.

He figured there were two main suspects in the scam: Jill, or, the likelier of the two, the tortoise. After all, it was his idea. Speedy could wait. He would interrogate the hare first.

Jill was still in a deep sleep when Billy and his minders arrived.

"Knuckles," he ordered, "throw those buckets of cold water over her. That will do for starters." She was, as far as he was concerned, partly to blame for him being so much out of pocket.

It took well over a half dozen buckets of water to wake her up; the cold water eventually bringing her to her senses. And by the look she saw on the bookmaker's face, she knew instantly that she was in big trouble. Without hesitation, she put the boot into Speedy.

"It was the tortoise, Boss. It must have been those mushrooms he gave me this morning. I thought they had a funny taste. Ever since, all I've wanted to do is sleep. I had nothing to do with any of it, Boss. Honest. It was that sneaky tortoise. He…"

"Shut it!"

Billy had heard enough. And, after getting a kicking from Knuckles, Jill was told to, "Get lost! Now!"

Jill didn't need a second invitation. She was off; this time in a reasonably straight line.

Knuckles was first to speak. "The tortoise couldn't have got far, Boss. It should be easy to get him. Even if we miss him, I know where he hangs out."

"Right," Billy ordered, "you and Nipper go get him. Don't damage him yet. Just bring him here. Right?"

He put on his 'or else' look.

"I want to talk to him first. Got that, Knuckles""

Reluctantly, the bulldog agreed. He had been looking forward to giving the tortoise a good hiding. "Whatever you say, Billy."

It didn't take the pair long to find the slow-moving Speedy. Disobeying his boss, Knuckles gave him a thump anyway, then picked him up and returned to where Billy had been waiting.

Chapter 5

With spring having now arrived, Anna the Anaconda, Albert's surrogate granny, was trying to get him to wake up.

"Albert. Oh, Albert, dear."

Still fast asleep, Albert looked around. Seeing no one, he returned to gnawing on the seventh – or was it the eighth? – dog's leg. He had lost count. Although a dedicated vegetarian, he found it difficult sometimes. Despite the hiccup in his make-up, he did still have some adder instincts, especially when asleep, and he would spend most of his dreamtime chewing on his friends, even though, when awake, no meat would ever, intentionally, pass his lips.

Once more, the voice called out, much louder this time, "ALBERT! ALBERT! Please wake up."

And once again, unable to locate the source of the voice, he returned to consuming the half-eaten dog's limb, though, to be honest, he was getting pretty bored with sodding dog legs. If he had to eat one more of the furry extremity he would scream. Fortunately, at least for this winter's hibernation, it was to be his last.

"ALBERT! I won't tell you again! Wake up!"

Granny Anna was beginning to get cross.

Albert stirred. Through half-closed eyes, he spied a juicy wriggling millipede dangling invitingly from Anna's mouth, not half an inch in front of his sensitive snout. And, despite spending the last five months munching on his friends, he was still hungry. And again, despite trying his best to be the committed vegetarian that all his forebears had been, down it went, along with the countless and delicious squirming drumsticks.

Immediately he regretted the transgression. If she had known, Granny Anna would have snatched the insect away, but, naturally, she had wanted to test his reactions, his reflexes.

Unfortunately for Albert, when they had first met, he had omitted to inform her that he wasn't a meat-eater. But accidents happen and he had been very hungry. "Granny Anna, please don't give me any more insects. I know it's strange but, if I can help it, I try my hardest not to eat meat."

Anna was amazed. A snake that doesn't eat meat! Well, it takes all sorts, she supposed. Still, if that's what the young snake was into, so be it.

While Albert had been asleep, Anna had put herself into semi-hibernation, only going out now and again to pick up a takeaway, so, the wildlife didn't suffer too much, apart from one or two slackers, who, unfortunately for them, weren't quite quick enough to scramble away. Now that Albert was wide awake, Anna needed to be sure that he was ready and alert enough to look after himself. Testing him with the arthropod earlier had been the ideal trial.

The den where Albert had taken his granny was the large hollowed-out tree he and his late mother had discovered. Luckily, Anna had joked, with the entrance facing south, it was perfect for catching the spring sun. She would love to see Albert go outside but was yet to be convinced that his blood had warmed sufficiently enough for him to look after himself. There was always the chance that a hungry predator could be waiting outside the log for anyone who was not alert enough to look after themselves. Adders are known to have several enemies, including foxes, which Albert, sadly, knows about already. Badgers and hedgehogs too are a danger. Birds of prey are also partial, now and then, to the unwary snake. Another danger is man, although the two rarely came into contact.

Albert needed to be on his guard all the time (nature, being a hard task master, didn't like lax creatures on her patch). He had to be alert, or else! He yawned, the zigzag patterns on his scales undulating as he stretched, his dark olive and brown markings in stark contrast to Anna's greenish-yellow and ovoid colouring across her back. Like most snakes, Albert picks up scents and vibrations using his forked tongue (in his case, unless he happened to forget himself, purely as a defensive measure); perfect for detecting any predator who wanted nothing more than to take a large chunk of him home.

He informed Granny Anna that he was ready to go outside. The early spring sun was beginning to burn away the last lingering shroud of early morning mist, and the warming of his blood enough for him to think about being off on his adventures once more.

Granny Anna was, not unlike most grannies, still a little concerned. And, if she was to be honest, really wanted him to stay in the den a little longer. Not because she didn't think he couldn't look after himself. Really it was for her. It was, after all, Albert who had indirectly given her a purpose, freeing her to begin a new life. And he would go some way in helping her get over any loneliness she would sometimes feel whenever she thought of her friends all those many miles away. And, of course, she could now catch her own food, rather than being fed, day after day, all those stale, 'best before yesterday' moth-eaten mice.

Albert called out once more; the excitement at being able to go outside almost too much. "Please, please, Granny Anna! I'm warm enough now!" he pleaded.

Anna sighed sadly. "Alright, Albert, but you just be careful. Do you hear?"

"Don't worry, Granny Anna," he assured her. "I will be okay."

With a wave of his tail, his tongue vibrating excitedly, he was on his way. Nervously, he slid into the warm sunshine. Sensing nothing close, he disappeared into the overlong grass and went looking for his pals.

The garden into which Albert slid was a mess; long since abandoned and now completely overgrown. Hardy daffodils and snowdrops fought a losing battle with the dandelions, chickweed and a host of other interlopers and unwanted wild plants. If the former owners had returned, they would, no doubt, have immediately taken the rotavator to the lot of them. Fortunately for Albert and his friends, this hadn't yet happened, and the over-abundant flora was ideal for hiding from the enemy. Predators.

Adjacent to the untidy garden was the abandoned cottage, now sadly in ruins and host to a variety of unwanted squatters, who, like the poor daffs and snowdrops, were all vying for space. Mice, reluctantly, had to share the accommodation with pigeons; neither group at all happy with the arrangement. The overfed birds were forever complaining about the comings and goings of the inoffensive tiny rodents. Apparently, their scuttling to and fro was stopping the obese birds getting in a decent night's sleep. And their incessant chatter, goodness, enough to send any bird batty! The rodents usually kept to themselves, not wishing to upset anyone. But, since the pigeons had moved in, and had started dumping on anything below that moved, 'coo, cooing' every time they scored a bull's eye, all the mice ever seemed to do was whinge. Still, the rodents had a point. All the pigeon crap that showered on them, all night – every bleeding night! – killed any thoughts of inviting friends around for a get together. The embarrassment of having to raid the local dump looking for discarded tin cans and wearing them as pigeon poop shields did absolutely nothing for one's image.

But what could you do when there was no landlord to complain to?

Chapter 6

Not far from the cottage was the ornamental pond; its only tenant a solitary fish, who constantly swam around and around, searching for someone – anyone – with whom she could have a sensible conversation. Luckily for the fish, the electricity supply to the circulating pump had been left on; the pump forever delivering oxygen-rich filtered water around and around. Perhaps whoever had lived there had felt sorry for the lonely fish. The aquatic vertebrate, knowing none of this, of course, continued her futile quest for real company. She was bored beyond belief with the resident frogs. All the warty amphibians ever wanted to croak about was what cute names they would give their offspring: "Alan", "Abigail", "Abner". On and on it went. "Zac", "Zelda" … Hour after boring hour. Day after bleeding day.

Albert had always loved this time of year; the sun just warm enough to keep his temperature rising steadily and, best of all, he would soon get to see his friends. (Hopefully they had all survived the winter.) First, though, some exercise. Cooped up in his den all winter, he needed to stretch himself, get his muscles moving. Setting off, he slid, first to his right, then sidestepped left. Next, he slithered around and around, before returning to his start point and finally raising himself, as if to strike in self-defence. Hopefully, all these seemingly random movements would persuade any prospective predator into believing it would be too much like hard work chasing such an agile quarry.

All of his activity was being watched. Maurice, a house mouse, had been resting behind a redundant molehill when he espied the adder carrying out his callisthenics. Normally he would not have dared leave the safety of his sanctuary during the daylight hours. Desperate to escape the non-stop complaints of the obese, incontinent and overhead crap factories, he had left the safety of the abandoned cottage and had a rare chance to remove his poo protector. (In his case, a very uncomfortable pilchard tin, which he had reclaimed from the local tip. Absolutely necessary, of course, unless you wanted to be covered in pigeon plop by the end of the night.) At least outdoors one wasn't forced to listen to the complaints; not to mention the constant pitter-patter of bird offal on the fish can. Unfortunately for Maurice, his day was about to get a lot worse than being covered in bird poo.

Albert's last leg (so to speak) of his exercises brought him to within a whisker of the rodent. Maurice, new to the area, and not knowing the snake's good nature, convinced he was about to be the adder's first meal of spring, fell into a dead faint. Feeling sorry he had frightened the tiny fellow into fainting, Albert tried nudging Maurice awake. When, at last, he managed to bring the poor lad back to consciousness, Albert gave him one of his trademark hellos: a big toothy grin. The glum mouse, once more, assuming he was a goner, collapsed again. This time, it seemed, for good. But this time Albert couldn't be bothered and quickly moved on, leaving the prostrate mouse to it. Well, after all, it wasn't his fault was it?

That's what he chose to believe, anyway.

Sliding past the ruined greenhouse, glassless now, he reached the old potting shed, also wrecked beyond repair; presumably demolished by the same gang who had broken all the glass in the greenhouse. The wreckage, though, allowed the abundant wildlife even more hiding places in which to shelter, giving both prey and predator an even chance of either feeding, or, better still, surviving.

Tongue vibrating constantly, Albert arrived at one of his favourite places – the pergola, now covered in an unruly climbing plant. It was a perfect refuge in which to rest and catch a little sun, warming his blood even more. Checking the coast was clear and nothing dangerous was close by, he closed his eyes.

He had just nodded off when, suddenly, he heard what sounded to him like a herd of demented elephants coming towards him, almost frightening him into shedding his skin. Seconds later, tiny, panic-stricken mammals, eyes out on stalks, streamed past him, round him, some even climbing over him, in their determination to escape whatever was chasing them.

Forked tongue vibrating madly, Albert located the source of their torment. Oh no, he groaned to himself. Not him! He kept his eyes firmly shut in a desperate attempt to pretend he wasn't here.

"HELLO!" an over-loud voice screeched.

It was yet another mouse; this time a dormouse. Albert had recognised the rodent's taste immediately and was amazed he had survived the winter. It was Lonely, the scourge of the meadow, also known by some as 'the doormouth'. Identical to other dormice, with the same rich orange/brown fur, bushy tail, blunt snout and large eyes, but that was where all other comparisons with his brethren ended. Whereas his brothers and sisters were quiet and wise enough to spend most of their lives in safety off the ground, only appearing in the evenings to feed, this mouse, throughout his entire young life, did everything to draw attention to itself.

Any sensible and vulnerable creature who was at the bottom of the food chain would have swiftly made themselves scarce, if they were unlucky enough to find themselves face to face with an adder; even an adder who happened to be feigning sleep. But, as we shall soon learn, 'sensible' and 'Lonely' do not appear in the same sentence. Anyone who had the misfortune to be anywhere close to this rodent – those who survived the experience – all agreed. He was about as welcome as a rat poison.

"HELLO!" the dormouse shouted, once again poking Albert hard on his nose. "ARE YOU ASLEEP, ALBERT?" As always doing his best to draw attention to himself. In fact, everything he did was over-loud: conversing, scrambling through the undergrowth, even sleeping. All things you would expect vulnerable creatures not to do to lure predators to themselves, he did. In spades.

Albert knew Lonely well; the story of the dormouse's upbringing and the struggles he had gone through as a youngster. Born last in a large litter, he was always going to be at the back of the queue when any food was dished out. But, as daft as he obviously was, he very quickly learned that loud meant getting attention, which in turn led to getting fed first, and nourishment meant survival. The downside to the non-stop noise was that the safety of the rest of his family was put in question, because, no matter how hard his parents tried, even after he was fed, they just couldn't shut him up. So, to ensure their safety – not to mention the family's sanity – the young dormouse was given his marching orders.

Banished from the nest and sent away to fend for himself, at a time when any immature rodent's survival depended on stealth and silence, he was still as noisy as ever. How he survived was a mystery, but survive he did. The noise he made alerted all shapes and sizes of predators. This was unfortunate for the ones who had felt sorry for him and those who befriended him, especially those who became victims. Learning very quickly, others, survivors, very soon realised that Lonely was a magnet for hungry predators and, for their own well-being, they all had to hide from him; he was just too dangerous to be near. Whenever the 'Lone Danger' came calling, they would be somewhere else. Fortunately for him, not so for the other vulnerable creatures, the local predators soon got the message. Whenever the daft mouse was around, all they needed to do was sit around, chatting, because it wouldn't be long before all kinds of tasty morsels came their way.

Sensibly, Lonely was permitted to roam free.

Albert, when he wasn't pretending to be asleep, was one of the few who would tolerate the lonely creature. After all, he knew what it was like to be an orphan (albeit, in his case, for about thirty seconds). Still pretending sleep, he decided to try to outwit the little mouse, keeping his eyes shut. Of course, it didn't work.

"ARE YOU STILL ASLEEP?" Lonely yelled once again, poking Albert on the nose once again.

Albert realised it was going to take something more radical if he were to rid himself of this pain in the backside. Perhaps he could frighten him into buggering off, conveniently forgetting he had already done to death one unfortunate mouse today. Baring his fangs, he pretended to bite the dormouse, stopping only when their noses touched. He didn't get the reaction he was expecting.

"YOU'RE FUNNY, ALBERT!" Lonely giggled, enjoying the game he thought he and Albert were playing.

The fluff I am!

"Don't you know what I am?" Albert assumed that his earlier hint would have helped. It did.

"OF COURSE, I DO!" the dormouse replied, somewhat taken aback with Albert's comment. "I'M NOT THICK, YOU KNOW."

Albert didn't know anyone who was only half as dense.

"WANT TO PLAY HIDE-AND-SEEK, ALBERT? Lonely wanted to know. "MY FRIENDS ARE ALWAYS HIDING FROM ME."

To get rid of the mouse, Albert lied. Yes, he would play. "But you will have to hide first." He had every intention of being anywhere but close to this idiot, once the annoying muppet was hiding, and the further the better.

The lonely mouse was ecstatic. At last he had someone who would play with him. "OH, ALBERT, YOU ARE MY BESTEST FRIEND, AND I DO LOVE YOU."

Albert wasn't at all impressed with the last bit. If any of his friends were anywhere near and had heard any of that his life wouldn't be worth living. He would have been mortified to know some of them were.

"Off you go, then," he encouraged his new best friend.

"WHERE SHALL I HIDE, ALBERT?" Lonely wanted to know.

"Suffering slug poo, mouse! I don't know!"

It was very rare for Albert to lose his temper and he immediately regretted his outburst.

Lonely began to sob.

"Oh, for the love of... why not try hiding near the potting shed?" He was beginning to regret not being a full-time meat-eater. Perhaps Lonely could be classed as a vegetable.

Surprisingly, the dormouse agreed. "YES, I COULD, COULDN'T I?"

Had the daft sod read his mind and was in favour of mouse-icide? No such luck.

"I'LL HIDE IN THAT BIG PLANT POT. YOU'LL NEVER FIND ME IN THERE, ALBERT."

With that, he was off, as noisy as ever, unaware of the panic he had caused to the tiny creatures; those who had been watching Albert embarrass himself. All of them forgetting the golden rule of survival: whenever the Plank of England was in the vicinity, make sure you were visiting relatives.

Albert, of course, wasn't to know, but, by suggesting that Lonely hid close to the potting shed, he may well have put the dormouse in a position to save his, Albert's, own life.

Hurrying away, keen to put as much distance between himself and the noisy nutmeg as possible, he tasted the air for signs of unfriendly alien life. Always a good idea, especially after being that close to the overloud rodent. Detecting only one other life form, not counting the mouse (and no one ever counted him), certain he had picked up the spoor of a friend, he went to say hello.

Chapter 7

The area Albert was headed for was the patio, which was normally the place where he and his friends met. Next to the patio was the large ornamental pond, and two of the characters he was certain to bump into when passing, and who never left the area, were the lonely fish, for obvious reasons, and Gnomez, a Mexican gnome. He had an even better reason for staying put. He was made of cement. Named Gnomez by the local creatures, only because, unlike most other gnomes who always insisted on wearing those ludicrous nightcaps, he sported a very fetching multi-coloured sombrero. A likeable chap; not least because he always had the good sense to keep his opinions to himself whenever Albert and his friends were making complete fools of themselves. Another and more likely reason, probably, was because his sombrero cast large shadows during the summer months, under which the more warmer-blooded friends of Albert could shelter.

Albert saw a creature he thought looked like his friend, Speedy; seemingly none the worse following his winter snacks. Although, he did seem somehow a little different. For a moment, Albert was at a loss. Then the penny dropped. Speedy didn't have a shell. He was naked!

"Been playing silly buggers again, I see," Albert began, making the bare-arsed tortoise jump.

The tortoise glanced up.

"Oh, hello, Albert. Erm, what makes you think that?"

"Well, you seem to be without your shell. Let me guess. You lost it on a bet?" He was furious. "How many times do I have to tell you?"

Speedy had been here before. The last time he and Albert had argued furiously. In the end, Albert had lost his temper and had threatened to eat him if he didn't stop, or at least slow down on the gambling. Not wanting to be eaten, even in jest, he had ducked back into his shell, refusing to come out.

Albert tried explaining to his best friend that he was only joking. But, no matter how hard he tried to explain, he, Speedy, had refused to listen. At least until Albert had properly calmed down and it was safe. He was about to pop his head back out when he heard Albert, now desperate, begin to apologise. He almost peed himself laughing, when he noticed that Albert had slid to the wrong end and had begun pleading for him to come back out so they could have a sensible face-to-face discussion. A very red-faced adder eventually heard him laughing, and only then realised he was apologising into his friend's backside. Speedy was warned not to make jokes about Albert being the only animal known to talk into an arse, as opposed to talking out of one. His.

Albert was not in the least bit surprised to see Speedy without his shell; his best friend's betting losses were legendary. This time, though, it looked as though he had gone too far.

"C'mon, out with it," Albert hissed. "What did you do this time?"

Speedy explained everything. First his expulsion from Billy's betting shop, then his hare-brained scheme to race a hare. Albert's jaw was beginning to drop. And how he had triumphed, and the money his family had won from the bookmaker.

"Everything was fine, until Jill the Hare grassed me up."

He then explained how the scam had unravelled.

"I had to promise Billy I would get him his money back, by yesterday. But, of course, I had already gambled the winnings away. Billy came round again and made his final demand to get his money back. He and his minders forced me out of my shell and threatened that, if he doesn't get his money, not only will I not get my shell back, he is coming looking for me, he says, to teach me a lesson."

It wasn't just the bookmaker threatening him with violence. Without the protection of his shell, Speedy was in mortal danger. He would be an easy meal for any half decent predator who just happened to be passing through the area. And, it wasn't until Albert had explained to him his vulnerability that Speedy began to grasp the seriousness of his situation.

"What do you think I should do, Albert?"

"Right," his pal began. "You have been lucky so far, but you aren't going to survive much longer if you stay visible."

Even with his help, it was going to be very difficult, almost impossible, for Albert to take care of his friend all the time, so something needed to be done, and quickly. First things first. A question.

"Have you got the money to pay him back? Yes or no?"

Speedy shook his head, no.

"Didn't think so. Okay, we will have to think of another way. It is Billy who has your shell? And do you know when he is coming back?"

Speedy again shook his head. Albert knew all about how nasty the bookmaker could be to non-payers and had heard all sorts of rumours. One of the more outrageous ones was how, as a youngster, Billy had savaged numerous hungry foxes, who were on the lookout for easy meals. Of course, he didn't believe any of it, but, just to be on the safe side, he needed to make sure Speedy was kept out of danger.

Like most other creatures, Albert had never seen a naked tortoise before, and for the last few minutes had, inadvertently, been staring at the naked tortoise's private parts. Red-faced he turned away, believing that it was Speedy who was embarrassed.

Speedy though could see that it was Albert who was uncomfortable, so, although he was in grave danger, he told one of his jokes. Unusually, even as a useless gambler, he was one of those characters who found it almost impossible to stay upset for long.

"Did you hear this one, Albert? Small boy says to his father, 'Dad, why are some women so ugly?' And his father replies, 'Oh, I don't know, son. Go and ask your mother'."

Albert giggled. Shell-less or not, Speedy was still a funny bugger. Nevertheless, he had to get him somewhere safe. Now. He looked around the patio for a suitable hiding place.

"Right, I want you to hide in that potato sack."

"You have got to be kidding me, Albert!" he complained. "No way am I going in there! It smells."

"Well, of course it does," Albert explained. "That's the whole point. It's to stop any of your agitated spoor from spreading."

Give me strength!

"Oh, right."

Speedy gingerly squeezed himself into the old sack, immediately sticking his head out from a hole in the side of the bag.

"Are you certain about this, Albert? It really does smell in here."

He was told to stop being a baby.

Taking one big gulp of fresh air, he ducked back into what he hoped would only be a temporary shelter.

Not wanting any passing predator to realise that there was an easy meal close by, Albert slid quickly away and went to see if he could find more of his and Speedy's friends. Together, they could perhaps think of a way to help get his friend's shell back. Most would already know the dangerous predicament the tortoise had got himself into. News of any animal's vulnerability travelled fast in Albert's world. For some, it could be their first meal of the day; for others, sadly, it would be their last. Speedy, like all defenceless creatures in the wild, would have to take his chances.

If he was to be honest, Albert didn't believe that his best friend stood much of a chance of making it through the rest of the day; what with his only protection, his shell, stolen, and Billy and his henchmen threatening to do all kinds of bad things to him later as well. Only if he was lucky enough to get his shell back would he be safe, and only then if he could stay out of Billy's way. That is, until the bookmaker had found someone else to terrorise.

Albert, his mind up, would do whatever it took to get Speedy his shell back. Now he had Speedy safely tucked away in the potato sack, it was up to him to do everything he could to save his friend. First things first though. He needed to get some of his energy back; otherwise he would be no use to himself, let alone Speedy.

It was a beautiful sunny day and his blood was as warm as it was going to get for this time of year. The local birds also, now that the sun was out again, began to get their enthusiasm for singing back. Male blackbirds competed loudly with one another for the somewhat dubious pleasure of trying to capture the hearts of the best-looking females, with some of the more desperate males even coming to blows. Most of them, though, just strutted their stuff, showing off. The females, of course, while secretly pleased to be the centre of attention, played it coy, refusing to have anything to do with what the boys had to offer. Until later that is, when it was time to help with the nest building.

Albert, who had quite a few feathered friends, listened for a while, trying to pick out a tune from someone he was acquainted with. One of the male blackbirds, upset after being given the elbow by his girlfriend, suddenly took flight. Believing it to be one of his chums, Albert raised himself off the ground, calling out "Good morning!"

Misunderstanding the gesture, surprised by the sudden appearance of an adder, the bird cried out in fright, depositing his recently digested breakfast on Albert's head.

"Thanks for that!" Albert called out to the now-liberated blackbird, grateful that there had been only one of the dirty sods. He hurried on before any more of the birds got the same idea and dumped more of the stuff on his head.

Chapter 8

Head now piled high with recycled bird poo, and keeping a wary eye out, Albert hurried away. After a short rest, he would go to the pond to get cleaned up, and then go and have a word with Mary. Perhaps she could advise him.

The creature Albert hoped could help him in his quest to keep his friend alive, at least until he got his shell back, was a slow-worm, called by others a 'blind worm', and, muddling things even further by some, a 'legless lizard'. She is the local mystic and psychic. Her professional name, the name she insisted on and was universally known by throughout the animal fraternity was 'Mystical Mary, Psychic Worm and Fortune Teller Extraordinaire'. She is also the local drunk.

Whoever had the foresight to name the species must surely have had Mystical Mary in mind. Legless by the middle of the afternoon, she was usually blind drunk by the evening. Therefore, two of the labels suited her perfectly; the third couldn't have been more wrong. 'Slow' she most certainly wasn't. Pleasant enough most of the time, her temperament quickly changed if her favourite tipple wasn't near to hand. On most occasions, even when meeting clients, she would always be close to being legless.

Whether sober or tipsy though, she always knew precisely what her customers were after. No matter how unlikely the outcome (given her clientele), they all needed reassurance, desperate to know what the future held for them, and the worm delivered, every time. No customer left dissatisfied, desperate to believe every word Mary fed them. Every one of her customers got what they wanted to hear. True or false.

Mary lived under a large broken plant pot, which was, conveniently, well placed under the meadow's sole apple tree. The shelter perfect in keeping her safe from the constant bombardment of air-to-surface missiles – windfalls – which could be deadly if you only happened to be six inches of skin and muscle. It was only when the overripe fruit landed and became soft and juicy that they became a danger to her; addicted as she was to the fermented fruit. From her first taste, she was hooked. Beginning on the odd sip, she was now slurping half a dozen or so fermented apples a day. Even so, her mind was still razor sharp, her constantly bloodshot eyes missing nothing.

After his short rest, with his blood now comfortably warm and most of his energy back, Albert slid towards Mary's plant pot. Sliding past a shard of broken glass, he caught a glimpse of himself. He was wearing a hat. Where the hell had that come from? Oh yeah, he'd forgotten all about dried bird poo. It was too late to do it now, but he must remember to wash it off after he had been to see Mary. He arrived at her plant pot and he could see from her sour expression that she had one of her infamous hangovers, and it looked like a big one. He wondered if he should give her a miss and divert to the pond. No, he decided. Her reputation for being a wise old biddy – drunk or hungover – was well-established. He would give her a try, if only for Speedy's sake.

Albert knew her reputation, though, so he had to be on his guard all the time, making sure that she didn't get him going with all that psychobabble rubbish. He would have to concentrate; not let her anywhere near his thoughts. Remember, you are only here to see if you can get help for your best friend. Mind you, he sniggered, it would be fun, while she wasn't at her hundred per cent best, if he had a little dig at the psychic's expense. Couldn't hurt, could it? Nah. Of course not.

"MORNING, MARY!" He called out as loudly as he could. Seeing Mary wince was, he thought, a good start. "What's the weather going to be like next week?"

"Watch it, Buster!" she warned, her headache suddenly getting worse. The last thing she needed was a smarty-arse adder trying to be clever. Out of habit, she enquired, "How can I help today, dearie? Don't tell me. I can see. You and your friend are in a bit of a dilemma."

Albert was taken aback. "Bloody hell, Mary! How did you know?"

"Mystical Mary, Psychic Worm and Fortune Teller Extraordinaire knows all, Albert."

She had long ago realised that anyone desperate enough to seek help from a permanently pixilated worm had to have a crisis of one kind or another, so everyone who came to see her got the standard, "How can I help today, dearie?" This convinced most customers they had come to the right psychic.

And it worked every time. She already knew all about Speedy's problems, so decided she would try to help, but not before Albert had been taught a lesson for shouting. Before that, though, to put him at his ease, she began with a little joke. "Do you want a drink, Albert? I thought perhaps we could get legless together!"

Albert completely missed the wisecrack.

"Erm, no thanks, Mary. That stuff makes me go dizzy."

"I know exactly what you mean, dearie."

She wasn't just being conversational either. Hiccupping, she tripped, lost her balance, and fell head first into one of the overripe fruit. With as much dignity as she could muster, she managed to extract herself from the apple as if nothing untoward had happened. Albert was beckoned to come a little closer. Mystical Mary Psychic Worm and Fortune Teller Extraordinaire was about to begin what she was famous for and to tie her latest client in psychic knots.

"Don't worry, Albert. Whatever you and Lonely have going, your secrets are safe with me."

Secrets? Lonely? *What the hell is she talking about? Oh bugger! He had forgotten about the mouse; she must have been watching him earlier.*

"No, No. Lonely just wanted to play with me."

Unfortunately, that came out all wrong.

"No, No. He was lonely, looking to me to be his special friend."

Sod it! That came out even worse. He thought it might be good idea to change the subject, divert Mary's attention to the bird droppings, his new head ware. Get himself back on the front foot again, metaphorically speaking. He tried: "What do you think of my new hat, then, Mary?"

"Looks like bird shit to me, Albert."

Worse was to come.

"Mind you, they say it's good for growing immature vegetables."

Unable to take that cruel put-down, and for the second time that day, he lost his temper. "Listen, you, you, legless maggot! Any more of your sarcasm and you'll end the day comatose, never mind slow!"

Not in the least worried by Albert's outburst, Mary, the know-all psychic, reinforced the fact that she was the best in the business by countering with, "I knew you were going to say that."

Unable to think of a nastier response, Albert asked for an unconditional ceasefire. "Sorry I called you a maggot, Mary. Truce?"

"That's okay, Albert. No harm done. Besides, some of my best customers are pupae."

It was true. Some of her clients were indeed all types and sizes of larvae; all of them desperate to be told they would turn into beautiful butterflies. The majority didn't, of course. Even so, Mary was astute enough to send them all on their way happy. All her customers left convinced that they had a bright and happy future, whatever the next stage metamorphosis brought. The happier the client, the greater her reputation as an all-seeing mystic.

Most of her mutated clients, sadly, would soon end up in the beaks of hungry birds, or even worse, a spider's web. Some would come to an even stickier end, once they had been being belted with yesterday's newspaper. This rapid departure from life always ensured that Mary never got any complaints, adding to her already exalted reputation. A lucky few would indeed turn into beautiful butterflies, often returning to the mystic to thank her. Some would even stay for a celebratory sip or two of her overripe apples. Quite often, red admirals could be seen hiccupping their way away from Mary's plant pot, having given up any attempt to fly.

She decided not to antagonise Albert anymore – for now anyway.

"What is it you think I can do for you, then?"

"My friend," he gave Mary a 'don't you dare' look, "has had his s…" He got no further.

"Shell stolen. Yes, I know. And you want my help to get it back, right?"

As a successful mystic, she had long ago realised that it would be good business if her customers believed she knew everything.

Albert's expression said it all. It hadn't occurred to him she knew already that someone had already told her.

Far cleverer than Albert would give her credit for, she moved on to the next phase.

"I will help you and Speedy, but I can't if you don't believe."

"Oh, I do," Albert lied.

He was not getting away with that.

"Right, repeat after me. I truly believe in the power of mind over the power of matter."

Power of the mind over power of the matter, my backside! Nevertheless (on the off chance she could help Speedy), he said he did.

Got him! Teach him to call me a maggot.

"Louder!" she commanded. "Not everyone heard your answer."

There was absolutely no further he would go.

"Don't push your luck, sister," he warned. He was getting pretty fed up of being on the wrong end of Mary's shitty stick.

Half drunk on apple juice Mary may well have been, but she knew when not to go over the top. How far she could go with her clients played a very large part in her success as a mystic. Sipping another mouthful of worm's ruin, she relented a little.

"Okay Albert," she began, "but there must be complete concentration from you. Otherwise I won't be able to see–"

"Any more of those and you won't be able to sta…" Not wanting another put-down, he quickly shut up.

"–into the future."

Then she fell over again.

Albert had been right. This wouldn't do at all. With Albert's assistance, Mary managed to get into an unsteady upright position. Feeling a little dizzy, she closed her eyes, which wasn't the most sensible thing she had ever done. The earth suddenly began spinning; much faster than it really ought to have done. Opening her bloodshot eyes, she realised that the earth hadn't moved; it was she who was doing the turning. To make matters worse, she now began to feel sick.

Albert was mesmerised by Mary's dance, assuming all her twisting and turning to be the prelude to the start of her psychic performance. Her spinning seemed to be having a hypnotic effect on him. He now was seeing her in a new light. Perhaps he had been over sceptical of her talents. He slid closer.

Spoiling this new-found belief, she threw up all over him.

Not in the least bit sorry she had just redesigned his camouflage, he was informed that it was better out than in and, to be honest, she didn't feel as ill or as off colour as she had a few seconds earlier. Which was more than could be said of Albert now, poor thing. He was furious with Mary, the dirty liquid lizard. That's a good one! Along with a few select swear words he would give that one a try.

Mary could see he was about to give her a mouthful and thought, I'll bet it wouldn't be half as colourful as the stuff I've just covered him in.

"Sorry Albert, but I must have complete silence. Otherwise the spirits will refuse to help."

She was a hell of a lot quicker that Albert could ever hope to be.

Dripping apple juice, he just had to do something in retaliation. Get some of his own back one way or another. A bite on her bum would do it of course. Just a little nip… Hang on, though! Wait just a minute! Getting his own back couldn't be easier. When she wasn't looking, he would pee all over her apples. Brilliant! He perked up immediately. A huge grin spread across his face.

Frightening the life out of him, she cautioned, "Don't even think about it."

Minds weren't the only things she could read.

Enough was enough. Desperate as he was to get help for Speedy, surely he had done his bit? So far, all he had got for his troubles was a verbal beating and covered in unwanted apple juice. Sorry pal, I did my best.

Making him jump, Mary called for him to keep concentrating if he was to help Speedy. Demanding everything and everyone in the meadow be silent and cease whatever they had been doing.

Lonely, who was still bellowing at everyone and anyone, now took this moment to take a breather. Not even Mystical Mary was going to shut him up for long; embarrassing Albert, with his "COOEE, ALBERT, I'M READY!"

The professional that Mary was, her smirk stayed hidden, insisting everything was still favourable and that Albert's friend was too far away to interfere with her 'psychic couplings', she again repeated her instructions. Albert was surprised and even Mary was a little shocked. The blackbirds had ceased their incessant chatter and the wind, which had only moments earlier been blowing quite strongly, died away.

An eerie silence settled over the meadow.

That was enough for Albert. Sorry Speedy, pal, I'm off.

Stopping him dead in his tracks, Mary ordered him to turn around, cease all his negativity and focus.

Hmph, he grumbled to himself. Pardon me for breathing! Then, remembering the psychic's earlier instructions, he silently apologised for his pessimism. Sorry, Mary.

Mary accepted his unspoken grovel. "Apology accepted, Albert. Now can we concentrate and see what can be done about getting Speedy's shell back?"

"It's about blooming ti…" he managed, before his bottle went.

Thus, what is about to happen would, very soon, become folklore. Not only among the psychic fraternity but also throughout the whole meadow; enhancing Mary's already exalted reputation, putting her on a par with a certain shell-less tortoise.

Chapter 9

Mystical Mary, Psychic Worm and Fortune Teller Extraordinaire, part-time soothsayer, full-time drunk, was about to become a legend revered by all. Everything she was about to forecast will come gloriously true, in the most spectacular fashion. As much a surprise to her as it would be to her slack-jawed customer. Only a heck of a lot quicker and a damn sight more accurate and painful than even she could have foreseen.

*   *   *

Wanting the next stage of the session to look as genuine as possible, Mary, once again, closed her eyes and, once again, lost her balance and for the third time fell flat on her face and, it seemed to Albert, fall fast asleep.

Well, he thought, that was a complete waste of half an hour!

He was about to move off when she woke up.

Explaining she hadn't been asleep at all but had been on a trip with the spirts in a search for his friend's shell, she could see from Albert's demeanour that he didn't believe her.

To keep him interested, she began moaning dramatically, reciting another newly made-up mantra: "Oh, Spirits of yesterday, Spirits of today, show me tomorrow, show me the way." She stole a sly glance at the open-mouthed Albert. She was quite pleased with herself. Usually, if she went on for as long as this with her regular clientele, they would have just buggered off.

Albert hoped he was far enough away not to get his mind, or come to that, his scales, readjusted.

"Albert, come closer," she instructed (he didn't move an inch), "while I'm re-psychling my inner thoughts."

"I wish you would stop recycling mine," he muttered.

It was now that everything began to change for Mary. From the tongue-in-cheek, just for a bit of fun, psychic, to a fully paid-up, bonified oracle. Suddenly she became stone-cold sober, more clear-headed than she had been for a long time, and her normally bloodshot eyes suddenly sharp and lustrous.

"The mists," she declared, "have cleared, and everything is coming through loud and clear. You have news for me? Yes! Thank you. Thank you."

Albert wondered who the hell she was talking to. It certainly wasn't him. Silly cow!

"Of course, it wasn't you, Albert. And another thing, I'm not a silly cow."

It wasn't only Albert who got the shock of his life; her reply even made her jump.

"Albert, I have just been told by the spirits that I am going to be visited by a stranger."

"Perhaps" Albert enquired, "you can ask whoever it is where the missing shell is?"

Mary wasn't listening. She was in a trance. Whatever was happening, she felt compelled to carry on.

"Albert," she enquired, "you don't have your brolly with you, do you? It's starting to rain."

Looking up at the clear blue sky, he was sorry, but he had left it at home.

Mary cried out in pain, "Have you just kicked me on the bottom, Albert?" she accused the startled adder.

He stared, open-mouthed. How the hell was he supposed to kick her? He would have liked to, if only to get his own back for covering him in apple waste earlier. Perhaps now would be a good the time to ask what the hell was going on.

The manic stare she gave him made up his mind. Perhaps not. The sooner he was away from this nut job the better. Just in case she had been listening in, he silently apologised, No offence, Mary.

"None taken, Albert."

Now where the hell had that come from? Mary was beginning to panic. (With her usual clientele, it had all been tongue-in-cheek readings.) Something very odd was going on here. Very odd indeed. She needed another a drink, and bloody quick! Just to be on the safe side, she had two. She began to feel light-headed again.

"Albert, apparently, I'm going on a short flight, free as a bird, up, up and away."

Before she disappeared, Albert enquired if on her travels she could keep an eye out for Speedy's shell.

Although she couldn't understand any of it, the panic she had had initially was now gone, and, apart from her sore bum, she was now beginning to enjoy the experience. Whatever was going on, she was on a roll. Suddenly, her migraine returned. Now what? And she was sure she could feel a lump on her forehead. For the life of her, she couldn't remember having collided with anything. Well, only when she fell, head first, into one of her overripe apples.

It eventually got through to her what Albert had said. Sod it! In all the excitement she had forgotten about the damn shell! Quick as a flash, she admonished him.

"If you'll just have a little patience! I am soaking wet, you know! Now, let me have another look."

Perhaps another sip of fermented apple juice would help.

"Right then, where am I…? Ahem, I mean… where was I? Ah, yes there it is."

Not having the remotest idea, not even caring now, she decided to play for time.

"Atishoo! Atishoo!" she sneezed.

All that rain, Albert thought.

"Yes, Albert. All that rain," Mary confirmed, reading his mind for what would be the final time.

* * *

The catalyst that would soon propel Mystical Mary, Psychic Worm and Fortune Teller Extraordinaire, part-time medium, all-star drunk, into a high-flying superstar had, for some time, been sniffing his way through the undergrowth, unseen and undetected by a mesmerised adder and a supposedly all-seeing, all-knowing semi-professional clairvoyant.

The game changer – a canine – had for some time been bursting for a wee and, as usual, had sniffed his way past numerous places he could have used to relieve himself. Beginning to think he couldn't hold back much longer, he, at last, found the perfect target: Mary. Raising his leg, he proceeded to pour the highly-pressurised pee all over the slow-worm.

"Argh! Phwa! Yuk!" Mary spluttered, pinned to the ground by the dog's high-powered liquid.

"Hoi, you," she managed eventually, "point that thing somewhere else, will you?"

The canine, having waited so long in happy anticipation of a moment just like this, was not about to aim elsewhere, or stop for that matter. And besides, as far as he was concerned, anyone who lived so close to the ground wasn't worth the effort. Every time the unfortunate Mary opened her mouth to protest, she got yet another squirt of the canine's redundant piddle. Finally empty, the mutt proceeded to carry out the technique countless canines had been doing for generations, and that was to vigorously scratch at the damp ground, not only distributing wet soil to all points of the compass but also back-heeling the soaking wet Mary – as she had so accurately predicted – squarely in the centre of her ample rump, launching her – again as she had forecast – high into the air.

Albert watched the show, relieved that it was someone else's turn to be presented with an unwanted waste product. Nor was he upset that the dog had launched Mary. Teach her to mess with my mind! All the same, he apologised to the flying psychic. And he was still no nearer to helping his friend find his shell.

The worm flew on, up, up and away, accelerating past a plant pot, calling out a good day to a startled vole, then, skimming over a small picket fence, she almost caused a mid-air collision between herself and a startled starling, who was just coming in to land. Luckily, the bird had seen Mary and had made an abrupt change of direction. Finally, gravity decided she was enjoying herself way too much and put a stop to her flight. Down she came, head-first into the hard ground, only just missing a scurry of startled squirrels. And, as everyone in the animal world knows, squirrels, not being the most subtle of creatures, immediately asked the dazed and winded slow-worm what was the first thing that went through her mind when her head hit the ground?

Mary, understandably not in the mood for small talk, lisped, "Only my arse."

Aided by friends, she managed to limp her way back to her upturned plant pot and her beloved ripe apples.

Albert, who had always thought flying to be the coolest of things to do and looked like it could be fun, changed his mind after witnessing Mary's unconventional take-off and her even more unorthodox landing.

The canine, inadvertently having helped Mary go some way to becoming one of greatest ever clairvoyants the meadow has ever known, sat down and had a good scratch. No ordinary member of the dog family, this canine came from royal stock: Captain Montague Montgomery Smythe IV, Cavalier King Charles spaniel, close cousin to the loyal companions of ancient Kings and Queens of England. And as such, believed himself to be superior to everyone, always insisting on talking down to each and all. Albert would be addressed as 'snake', with a small 's', and Mary, if she hadn't been so bloody accurate, would have been addressed as 'worm', with an even smaller 'w'. The first-class snob that he was, the Cavalier King Charles never deigned to use one word where ten would sound intellectually classier to anything the peasantry could muster. Not surprising, most of the time, none of his friends, including Albert, could understand what the hell he was talking about. Still, he was tolerated among Albert and all his friends; not least because he could always be relied upon to be wound up easily.

Already forgotten was his part in the rapid disappearance of the slow-worm. He wished Albert a good morning. "Salutations on this resplendent vernal equinox, snake."

As usual, Albert had no idea in what language he had been spoken to. Nevertheless, he greeted the King Charles, "Good morning, K.C."

The ultimate snob, it would never have occurred to the spaniel that his friend was being anything but subservient in using the royal initials. However, as everyone but the spaniel knew, it had nothing to do with rank, title or privilege, nor was any grovelling involved, but everything to do with the fact that the royal spaniel always seemed to have either his nose or his backside jammed in the pavement gutter. Hence his nickname, 'K.C.': 'Kerb Crawler'.

"Acquired any fortune regarding that damnable tortoise carapace yet, snake?" Albert was incomprehensively asked.

Except for the word 'tortoise', Albert had absolutely no idea what K.C. had said, but he guessed the spaniel had asked after Speedy's shell.

"No luck yet, I'm afraid, K.C."

K.C. sniffed the smell radiating from Albert, who hadn't yet had time to wash off someone else's waste product, was rank. The King Charles, descended as he believed from royal stock, was used to the lower classes being anything but clean, but, for goodness sake, snake, doesn't one ever wash? He decided not to tell Albert what he thought about his personal hygiene – for now – as there were more pressing subjects to discuss. He would keep his powder dry. Perhaps, when the time came to pee again, he could give the bounder a good hosing down.

"Jolly bad show. Chap losing his home like that, what! Suffice to say, old boy," he continued, "anything one can do to alleviate the conundrum, one only need enquire."

After all the excitement Albert had just been through, he was now beginning to tire, and needed to rest and warm up again. Getting rid of the spaniel was easy. Knowing K.C.'s organisational skills, Albert concocted a meeting for later. Get all their friends together and perhaps come up with some ideas to help Speedy, which, when he thought about, as it happened, wasn't such a bad idea anyway.

"Resplendent suggestion, snake. You are going to require a presiding officer, of course. That, quite obviously, will be oneself."

Albert looked lost.

"Someone in charge. Me, man! Me! For goodness sake, snake! Get a grip!"

Perhaps it hadn't been such a good idea after all.

"No gratitude needed, snake. One does have to carry out one's duty, don't you know? No offence intended, old chap, but one needs to keep you ruffians in place, what? Wouldn't do to allow to let the peasants get above their station, now would it? Minutes of the assembly to be taken, of course. One does need to chronicle all proposals and suggestions."

Albert looked lost.

"Keep records, snake. Keep up, will you, man?"

Albert was beginning to wonder what the hell he had got himself into.

"I will arrive precisely at two o'clock, snake. And I expect you to inform all and sundry not to be dilatory. Got that?"

Albert was beginning to wish it had been he who had been launched.

Even now, K.C. wasn't quite finished.

"Never let it be said that Captain Montague Montgomery Smythe IV, distant cousin to the loyal companions of the Kings and Queens of England, never went to the aid of a fellow creature in difficulties."

At last, the spaniel turned to go.

"Oh, by the way, do not forget, snake, fourteen hundred. Toodle-pips, old boy."

Fourteen hundred? Toodle-pips? What the hell was a toodle-pip? And why would he want fourteen hundred of the bloody things? He considered calling K.C. back to explain. Sensibly, he thought better of it. He was too late anyway. The canine had already left; no doubt looking to pee on and launch another unfortunate victim into the stratosphere.

Desperate – after the goings-on of the last hour – to get some of his energy back (yet again, having a wash would have to wait), he headed towards the old shed, where he could see an upturned wheelbarrow; its shiny metal wheel, minus the rubber tyre, revolving rapidly in the wind. First, though, a small detour to see how Speedy was doing. About to call out, he could hear snoring. Speedy was asleep. Deciding to let his friend have his nap, Albert slid silently away. He passed the large plant pot where Lonely was hiding and, careful not to let the noisy dormouse catch sight of him, he slipped quickly under the barrow. With the sun heating the metal, his body temperature would quickly return to normal and remain high, not allowing his blood to get too cool, and at the same time the upturned shelter would hide him, safe from the prying of hungry predators.

Testing the air once again, he got the all-clear, safe, not only from his natural enemies but also from his un-natural friends. They were doing his head in.

Chapter 10

As was usual for this time of year, rabbits, after a couple of months chilling out, emerged from their burrows; the warm spring sunshine perfect for topping up faded fur. Then, while bucks chatted about this year's bunny hopping championships, the ladies discussed what new fur style was in, and what was 'so last year', before deciding who was the best fur dresser to use. After all the appointments had been booked, and the boyfriends had been given their orders, it was down to the meadow to watch the annual Mad March Hare boxing championships. Every year, it was the same. Flat-nosed jacks knocking seven bells of fluff out of each other; all for the painfully dubious pleasure of being first in line to date, they hoped, the best-looking jills. Normally, anywhere else but in this meadow, it was the female and the male who went hell for leather when picking partners, but, in this strange place, the males had long ago decided hitting a lady ungentlemanly. The truth, though, was somewhat different. There was no shame in losing a boxing bout to your male counterpart, but being beaten year on year by the – supposedly – weaker sex was, to say the least, mildly embarrassing. Unfortunately, for the jacks, this year as last year, and the year before that, all they again got was the proverbial brush-off, leaving them frustrated, bruised, battered and bleeding. However, being the optimists they were, the jacks believed that this time it would be different, begging and pleading with the unsympathetic jills to, please, have some compassion.

"After all," as one of the rejected hares complained, "what the hell else is there to do around here, at this time of year?"

All the rabbits agreed. Hares were clearly insane.

*   *   *

As suddenly as the wildlife had appeared, they just as quickly vanished. Billy the Bookmaker and his henchmen had arrived, and they were looking for trouble. As far as everyone was concerned – rabbits, hares and most other creatures – he was bad news.

Unfortunately, one of the male hares, still to recover after being on the wrong end of an earlier good hiding, and who wasn't fully alert, wasn't quite fast enough to escape and was cornered and trapped.

"Where's Speedy?" Billy wanted to know.

"Who? I don't know."

Still dizzy from his earlier assault, the hare had no idea what Billy was talking about. A thump on his twice-broken nose helped convince him otherwise.

"I don't know where he is. Honest."

He was given another thump for his honesty.

"Not good enough," Billy warned. "What do you think, boys?" he asked his two compatriots. "Do we believe him?"

"Give him another thump, anyway, Boss," the more violent of his companions suggested.

"Mmm, I've got a better idea."

Billy shoved his nose into the face of the terrified hare.

"Right you! If...no, WHEN you see Speedy, you tell him he has got until five tonight to get my money. Got that?"

The terrified hare nodded as vigorously as he could. Yes, yes, yes, he had. The hare turned to go but Billy wasn't finished with him just yet.

"And you tell him, if he can't, or won't, pay me, then the first thing to happen is his shell gets flattened. Got that?"

Another series of nods confirmed he had.

"Then, if that doesn't persuade him, he is dog food. Right, boys?"

"Right, Boss." Two voices, both snarling, both in agreement.

Billy, now dangerously polite, explained to the hare, "Please get the message to the tortoise, okay? If not, well, the boys know where to come for their dog food. Right, lads?"

His meaning was crystal clear.

Once again, the two voices growled in unison. "Right, Boss."

"Okay, you," he ordered the terrified hare, "on your way. And don't forget, the tortoise. Or the boys will be back."

This time the hare was allowed to get away.

"Okay," Billy announced, "all this talk about food has made me hungry. Let's go eat."

The trio departed just as quickly as they had arrived. You could almost hear the sigh of relief from all the creatures in the meadow.

A short time later, a hungry hedgehog, awoken earlier than usual, thanks to the noise the hares had been making, had left her winter shelter to look for a snack, and, after a quick search of the meadow, she espied two unvigilant earthworms, themselves not yet fully awake. She listened for a while to the discussion the pair were having on what the acidity in the soil had been doing to their delicate segments, before pouncing on the nearest, bringing an abrupt end to their debate. The surviving worm, forgetting all about her flaky membrane, dived head first back into the soil. There were worse things in this life than having rough skin.

*   *   *

Albert, warmed up by now, was about to slide to the pond to clean himself off when something happened. Something, which, for now, made him forget all about his ablutions. He could taste something different, and for the moment couldn't quite put his tongue on it.

It was alien pheromones, but, as far as he could tell, friendly pheromones. Another snake, Sadie, a female adder, had been giving off her scent, desperately trying to attract Albert's attention. Albert hadn't known, of course, but for a long time Sadie had been watching him from afar and had become besotted. Living in the neighbouring meadow, but never wanting to encroach on his patch – until now – she decided it was about time she introduced herself to the handsome adder. Her sisters, though, had warned her again and again about Albert and what an idiot he was, and it would be a good idea to stay clear of the buffoon. But, like all younger siblings, she, of course, knew better.

Albert was being driven crazy, her eye-catching zigzag pattern adding to her allure. Though it mattered little to him what colour she was. It was her perfume and it was driving him crazy. He slid closer to Sadie, wondering what the heck was going on and what happened next. Sadly, with the sudden loss of his mother, and never able to get a sensible word from his grandad, he was never taught how to go about wooing a girlfriend.

Giggling, in the belief that Albert was just playing hard to get, Sadie decided to tease him and began to slide away.

He did the first thing that came into his mind and lashed out with his tail, catching Sadie a glancing blow. She lashed back, seemingly in retaliation, then began to accelerate away ever faster. This was, of course, all part of the courting ritual and he was meant to chase after her.

What the...! Had he upset her already? Had he inadvertently done something wrong? Probably not. More likely, it was the smell emanating from him that was putting her off. With everything that had been going on today, he had still to wash off the blackbird poo and Mary's redundant apple juice. Surprised, he could see that she hadn't buggered off, and he saw her hiding in the long grass. Setting off again, he tried to close the gap.

Giggling, Sadie put on a spurt, widening the distance between them. She was enjoying herself.

Now what the hell was she doing? Surely, she hadn't jilted him already? Ever since he had woken up that morning, everything, seemingly, had conspired against him. Shouted at by a mouse, crapped on by a bird and covered in redundant apple juice by a worm. Enough was enough! He decided to cut his losses and go and see how Speedy was getting on.

On his way to see Speedy, he slid past Sadie, hiding in the long grass, and once again her pheromones began to surround him. Then things began happening. Things that were completely alien to him. He could feel himself getting an erection. He was stumped, for a moment, then – nature being what it was – everything began to fall into place. He was beginning to catch on.

He espied Sadie. Setting off once again, he began to inch closer.

To stimulate Albert even more, she again pretended she wanted nothing to do with him, accelerating as did he. He was now getting into the swing of things, catching on, although, frustratingly, he didn't seem to be closing the gap. Typical! he thought. Now having worked out what to do, I can't catch up to do anything about it!

He was about to put in another sprint when, having only just come to terms with the discovery that he had a penis, he got an even bigger shock. He could feel two! What he is about to discover – and what his grandad should have remembered to tell him – is that adders have two internal penises, both of which, until mating is imminent, remain inside the body and only then do the two members appear. Albert, of course, knows none of this.

Two! Two? What do I need two for? Thirty seconds ago, I didn't know I had one! So, what the hell am I going to do with two? Perhaps, he reasoned, we adders are born with two. He was, again, no thanks to his bloody grandad, just about coming to terms with the facts of his life.

Then, if discovering he had new appendages sprouting out all over the place wasn't bad enough, another horrifying thought occurred to him. How the hell do I choose which one goes first? And what if the one going second goes into a sulk and refuses to co-operate? His head was beginning to spin again. Perhaps the pair, from the outset, had already discussed as to who was to go first and which of them had to wait its turn? Sod it! He would have to worry about all that later.

Having seen the nude Speedy earlier, he assumed his own would be no different, apart from having two. Curiosity eventually getting the better of him, he looked and down and saw… Nothing. He was penis-less. He almost fainted. Bugger! Two of the sods and I've lost them already!

He screeched to a halt; all thoughts of courtship gone. Not unreasonably he thought, he had to get them back. Doing an immediate about-turn, he began a search of the garden. First left, then right and back again, he scoured the whole area. Nothing. Devastated and about to give up, he saw movement in the grass. There, not three feet away. He called out. Desperate for the pair of penises to return, he began pleading with them, begging for them to, "Please, please, come back!" Sadly, for Albert they just weren't interested.

Still in shock, when he thought things couldn't get any worse, the digits began to dig themselves into the hard ground. As desperate as he was for the pair to return, they seemed just as determined to escape. He was too traumatised to realise he had just scared the living daylights out of two terrified earthworms. How on earth could he explain his predicament to Sadie? She would be so disappointed.

A dejected adder slithered slowly towards the female. However, the nearer he got to his girlfriend, the stronger her pheromones became. Suddenly, he realised that that warm feeling had returned. His erections were back. Perhaps, he thought, the pair had felt sorry for him, or, more likely, had decided that the earth at this time of year wasn't warm enough for them and had reattached themselves when he wasn't looking. It was still okay to carry on. But just to be on the safe side he refused to look down.

Confidence returning, and with renewed determination, he moved into overdrive.

"Coming, Sadie," he called, before catching his tail on an old garden trowel and falling over.

Undeterred, he set off once again but, unfortunately, he lost sight of Sadie. Raising himself just to get his bearings, at the same time accelerating, he slammed head-first into the tyre-less wheel of the barrow, jamming himself into the empty groove of the wind-driven, rapidly revolving, circular disk. Wedged firmly and solidly, he began accelerating round and round, faster and faster; his world now a dizzy blur of speeding scenery. No matter how hard he tried, all his attempts to free himself came to nought.

Although Sadie thought he was showing off that little bit too much – a bit over the top – she was entranced. The young female snake was flattered that Albert would go to so much trouble just to impress her. She couldn't wait to see what he did for an encore.

Perhaps a couple of dozen revolutions later, Albert's head, at first immovable, began to work itself loose. Now, he thought, if he could only free the rest of his body, he would be able to get off this damn roundabout. It was a lot easier than he had anticipated. Launching him into the air, the rapidly revolving wheel ejected its unwanted substitute tyre. Head to the front, as straight and as swift as any bolt shot from a crossbow, away Albert flew, higher even than Mary; only twice as quick.

Sadie loved it, calling out as Albert went higher and higher, "Yeah, Albert! Yeah!" His impression of a Catherine wheel had been amazing, but his aerobatic gymnastics? Wow! Albert, she thought, was going to be a fun snake to be with.

Stunned, Albert flew over the fishpond. Fortunately, it wasn't going to be a very long trip. Even before he could think to ask himself what the hell he was doing up here, he was on his way back down again. He would have followed the same flight path Mary had taken earlier had it not been for a stroke of luck. His tail, catching on a wild shrub, changed the direction of his unintentional and unwanted trip.

It wasn't until she saw the look of sheer horror on his face that Sadie realised he hadn't been showing off at all. All too soon he was on his way down, hurtling directly towards her, making escape from the unguided missile that was Albert impossible. Maybe sliding to her left would be safest, then perhaps going right would be best, it was no use. There was only ever going to be one outcome. She closed her eyes and waited for the inevitable collision.

Down he plunged, belly first. With all the subtlety of a brick, he landed, almost flattening poor Sadie. "OOMPH," was the only word she could muster, as the breath was squeezed from her tiny lungs.

Still, Albert wasn't finished. Rebounding off the wounded female, up he went again, this time coming down tail first, poking her in the eye.

"OW!" she screamed.

Unable to see properly for a second, she began shoving Albert away, desperate to extract herself from the lunatic's unwanted embrace. After what seemed to her an age, she managed to extricate herself. All thoughts of romance swiftly evaporated. Gasping and panting, she managed to get back much-needed oxygen into her deflated lungs. Just enough to be able to tell Albert to bog off, leave her alone and, for goodness sake, go and have a wash! Unfortunately, the only understandable utterance was a gasp, followed by a raking cough.

Misunderstanding, believing she wanted a cigarette, Albert apologised. "I'm sorry, my dear. I don't smoke. And if you want my advice, you sound as if you should give it up to."

If looks could have killed, he would have been a burnt roast.

Albert wasn't in the best of conditions himself. Ever the optimist, though, he hoped that Sadie hadn't noticed anything amiss. Well, not all first dates were perfect, were they? Sadie agreed, and vowed to herself that there was no prospect of a second either. She was going home. No matter how desperately keen she had been to get to know Albert better, it was now not going to happen. Not if she had anything to do with it, it wasn't. No matter how desperate she had been to have a family. Not with Albert it bloody wasn't.

Reaching the dividing line between the two meadows, having got all of her breath back, she turned, calling out, "My sisters were right. They always said that if your brains were made of dynamite, you wouldn't have enough to blow the top of your head off!"

A cheap shot? Of course, it was. But it went a little way into making her feel just that little bit better.

Mishearing the cruel jibe, still somewhat disorientated from his earlier mishap, Albert, chest puffed up, replied, "Yes, you are right, my dear. All my friends think so too."

Chapter 11

When, from the very beginning, Albert began making a fool of himself, shouts of derision came from all corners of the meadow: "You don't know what you're doing!" That put-down, though, changing to "We know what you're up to!" once Albert had, at least to the watching audience, looked like he had got the last part of the courting ritual right. All of the onlookers enjoyed the show he had been putting on for them. His audience all agreed that the snake was always good for a laugh.

Albert only heard the final chorus of the chants and, assuming his friends had been congratulating him, he slid over to thank the well-wishers. Assuming he was upset with them, the whole group fled. Perhaps there was another predator close by, and he would have been certain, had he not heard giggling and sniggering coming from various parts of the garden. He sighed. What do they know anyway?

But he was honest enough to admit to himself, his first date hadn't gone down that well. Perhaps next time?

He decided to see how Speedy was coping. With all the goings-on of the last hour or so, his friend probably thought he had deserted him. Calling out his name, Speedy popped his head out from the potato sack. Albert didn't get the welcome he expected.

"You smell worse than this sack, Albert! And what the hell are you wearing?"

"Don't you start!" Albert warned his friend. "Anyway, I was on my way to get cleaned up."

He explained that he, Speedy, needed to stay hidden a little longer.

"K.C., I think, is getting everyone together for later, so, hopefully, we can work something out. So, you stay where you are until I call you, okay?"

"Alright. Thanks, pal."

Speedy quickly ducked back into the potato sack. It didn't smell as bad as Albert.

Albert slid along the patio and towards the pond. Speedy was right. He did smell. It was way past time he washed all the smelly gunk off. Submerging himself in the cold clear water, the bird waste and Mary's unwanted stomach contents began to dissolve and break up.

The koi carp watched Albert from beneath a lily pad. At four years old, she was well into her prime; her scales a kaleidoscope of different hues and shades. Sadly, she was the sole survivor after a vicious attack by a pair of greedy herons, who had reduced the pond's population from a busy nineteen to just the one. Harmless (shortened to 'Armless' by angry frogs, after she was observed devouring a few wayward tadpoles). Although a bit miffed that he had decided to wash all that muck off in her pond, she wished him a good morning, deciding to keep her angry retort to herself; instantly changing her mind when she accidentally swallowed a mouthful of bird droppings.

"ARGH!" she spluttered, spitting the larger lumps out. "Ooh, I do hope you are feeling better now?"

The sarcasm was completely lost on Albert, for, although Armless understood perfectly what was being said to her, her replies never get beyond watery blubbles, burps and blurps.

Now clean and out of the water, Albert politely greeted the fish. "Good morning, Armless. Lovely day, isn't it?"

"Yes, it is, Albert," the koi just as politely replied. "Blubble, Blurp, Bubble, Burp." Four watery speech blisters floated gently to the surface, each bursting one by one.

Albert waited impatiently until the last blister of her speech bubble had disappeared, before asking the carp if she had heard about Mary's flight.

The koi carp blubbled, "Yes, Albert, I have. Everyone's talking about her."

Not understanding a single word, if indeed that's what you could call them, he nevertheless plodded on. Now he began to shout. Having once been told that, when speaking to someone whose language you don't understand, the best thing to do for both parties is to yell. "HAVE YOU HEARD ABOUT SPEEDY'S BAD LUCK?" he bawled.

"Yes, I have," she replied. "If there is anything I can do to help, all you need do is ask," she blubbled. "And Albert, please, stop shouting. I'm not deaf, you know."

His yelling echoed around her pond, giving her a headache.

Unwittingly, he thanked her for her offer. "YES, IF YOU CAN THINK OF ANYTHING TO HELP, WE WOULD BE GRATEFUL." He then asked after her health. "HOW ARE WE TODAY? WELL, I HOPE?"

"No," she sneezed. "Atchblubble. As you can hear, I'm not very well at all."

Her cold, which she'd had all winter, was still to clear up. Explaining her predicament, she said, "Thank you for asking, Albert, and for being considerate. Not like those rude and smelly frogs. I haven't been well all winter and could do with cheering up. I…"

She got no further. Once more completely oblivious to what she was complaining about, Albert yelled, "OH, WELL. JUST SO LONG AS YOU ARE HAPPY."

With that, he slid quickly away. He had something much more important to deal with.

Armless wasn't at all impressed, abruptly changing her mind. He wasn't as nice as she had first thought, sliding away like that. Not even a goodbye or a 'Bless you'. Sneezing once again, and in somewhat of a sulk, she swam over to a string of frog spawn, wiping her nose on the jellified tadpoles.

"Dirty cow!" several hundred tiny voices squeaked in complaint.

Choosing to ignore their tiny protests, she glided back to her lily pad to await the return of their absent parents, who would, no doubt, complain about the colds she had allegedly infected their Lilliputian offspring with. She sneezed once more; her cold didn't seem to be getting any better. In a bit of a huff, she swam over to the mini tadpoles again, this time deliberately sneezing all over the immature frogs, "ATCHBLUUBLE." Hopefully, the older frogs caught her cold. "Thod 'em!" she grumbled. It wasn't easy having a cold and being damp all the time.

On the patio was another of Albert's friends. He too seemed to be having a pointless and one-sided conversation; only his was with Gnomez, the Mexican gnome. It was 'Prof', the local, feathered version of a hippy. Prof was a male blackbird and, like all male blackbirds, had jet black plumage, with what had previously been a bright orange bill; now stained dark green. Never without a fresh blade of grass in his beak (the grass he constantly chewed came from any newly mown lawn. Although he would never admit to it, it tasted like cold spinach), but he was – as they say – 'cool' and laid back. He even had small beads attached to his overlong feathers. How he flew was a mystery to everyone. Usually spaced out, he inevitably began his conversations with "Peace, man."

Well-liked by Albert and his friends, he was yet another whose words needed to be deciphered carefully. "Peace, man," being one of the very few pre-decoded sentences Prof ever uttered. All other remarks were aphorisms, sayings and proverbs. Hence his nickname 'Prof'. Proverbs were his thing.

Seeing Albert approach, Prof called out a greeting, "Hey, Albert! Peace, man. How's it swinging?"

"Cool, Prof." (Albert had been here before.) "You're looking good, man."

The blackbird immediately contradicted him. "Appearances can be deceptive, bro."

Albert, it seemed, didn't know anyone who could speak in first-time English. Nevertheless, he liked Prof, so would give it a go.

"Anything I can do to help, Prof?" he enquired kindly.

"Every Jack should have his Jill, Albert," Albert was informed.

That one was easy. Perhaps Prof had decided to speak English, for a change.

"Ah, anything I can do to help?" he again enquired kindly.

"A civil question deserves a civil answer, bro," the bird promised, informing Albert. "The female of the species is deadlier than the male, man."

What the hell has the postma... Oh yeah. Oh well, back to trying to decipher the bird's quiz words. He thought about that one for a second, then had a guess and asked the downbeat bird if had he been dumped by his girlfriend.

Confirming Albert's shot in the dark, Prof replied, "Promises are like pie crusts, man. Meant to be broken."

It sounded to Albert like Prof needed a little encouragement to move on, and so he tried a maxim of his own. Getting it completely arse about face.

"Never mind, Prof," he claimed. "When one door opens another is sure to slam in your face."

The blackbird's sour look brought him swiftly back to earth.

Humph! Try to help someone and what do you get? That's the last time I try to console you, mate!

What Albert wasn't to know, Prof did appreciate his attempt to cheer him up, and said so. "Many are called Albert, but few are chosen. Thanks, man."

In a little bit of a huff, Albert was about to slide away, when, "Psst, Albert. Over here." It was the hare Billy had threatened earlier. "Quick!"

He slid over to where he saw the hare hiding in the bushes.

"Hello," he greeted the newcomer. "Have you come to help Speedy?"

"Sorry, Albert, no, but I do have a message for him from Billy the Bookmaker."

The hare was obviously worried, not knowing what reaction he would receive from the snake when he passed on the message.

Albert told the hare not to worry and to relax.

"Well, I know you and Speedy are best friends, so I thought you could pass the message on?"

Albert nodded.

"If Billy hasn't got his money by five tonight, Speedy will not see his shell again. And he said that wouldn't be the end of it either, and you know what that means, Albert."

He certainly did.

"Do you know where Billy is now?"

"Yes, I do, Albert. He and his minders went for their lunch."

The hare was getting more and more nervous, looking around, as if he believed Billy was about to leap out of the bushes.

He hurried on.

"And I know it's the same place he keeps all his trophies. That's where, I'm certain, your mate's shell will be."

He then went on to explain the exact location where he knew Billy to be.

"I'm sorry I'll have to go, Albert. If Billy finds out I've told you where he is, I'm done for."

Albert thanked him and assured him that yes, he had helped Speedy.

"Best go now, and thanks again."

He would have to warn his friend to be on the lookout. He slid over to the potato sack to warn Speedy not to move. He was about to call out when he heard snoring; the tortoise had gone back to sleep. Deciding to leave him, he made up his mind to get his own head down for a few minutes to reheat himself. Before he did so, however, he slid across to warn a couple of early arrivals what he had just been told by the hare and to ask them to keep an eye on Speedy for a couple of minutes.

"Okay, Albert," the gathering mammals agreed. "If he wakes up, we will tell him to stay where he is."

Reassured, he slipped away, first making sure that he wasn't exposed to any danger of assault. Before he dozed off, however, he listened for a while to the conversation Prof thought he was having with Gnomez the Mexican gnome, about the advantages of chewing on freshly mown grass. Smiling to himself, he slowly slipped into a light sleep.

His daydream of multiple tongues slobbering over him and cold wet noses getting intimate with his backside seemed very realistic. One particularly cold nose, stuck halfway up his bum, jolted him awake to find he hadn't been dreaming at all. K.C. the King Charles spaniel had arrived and he was just in time to see it lifting its leg and about to give him the promised hosing down.

Chapter 12

For the second time that day, he was lucky to have escaped being half-drowned in unwanted pee. Already dumped on, by a loose-bowelled bird, and covered in unwanted apple juice by an inebriated slow-worm, he was in no mood to be immersed in dog urine.

"Oi, you," he warned, "watch where you pour that stuff!" He was convinced the mutt went around urinating on as many acquaintances as he could get away with.

"Ahem, sorry old boy. Apologies. Didn't see you there," the spaniel lied. "Force of habit, what?"

K.C. wasn't the least bit sorry, peeing on the local peasants being very low on his priorities of what not to do today.

"You will be, if you try that again, mate!" Albert warned.

Above all that fisticuff nonsense, K.C. informed Albert that he was off to complete the organisation of his gathering. Albert gave him the usual blank look.

"The meeting? Repatriating the shell? Oh, for goodness sake!" And with that, off he went.

Passing the blackbird, K.C. wished Prof a good morning. "Exemplary conditions for this phase of the season, my good man, what?"

Prof got in his own piece of gobbledegook. "If tha wants owt done, K.C., do it for thee sel."

Neither of them had any idea what the hell had been said.

*   *   *

Meanwhile, thanks to K.C.'s organisational skills, all manner of small and large creatures arrived to give their support to Speedy. Quite a few of the arrivals were gamblers themselves, all knowing the predicament he had got himself into – one or two having once or twice been in the same boat as the now naked tortoise – and all were willing to help in any way they could. As always, nothing stayed secret for long in the meadow. Some, those who had been jeering and then cheering Albert earlier, nervously made their way towards him. Never one to hold a grudge, his philosophy being live and let live, he greeted them all, even stopping for a chat, remarking on Mystical Mary's fortune telling ability, having the foresight to see into her own future. One or two had even been to see her, explaining (tongues firmly in cheeks) that, apart from having to drink apple juice through a straw and talking through her bum, she was fine.

After sliding around, warning them all about the danger from Billy, Albert stopped for a while to watch K.C. scampering around, trying to make an impression on the gathering crowd.

He was about to slide over to the potato sack, when the earth suddenly began to shudder and tremble beneath him. What the hell is that? An earthquake? Even more frightening, and without any warning, a mini-mountain began to grow. The mound of earth grew and grew, until, suddenly, almost frightening everyone to death, the volcano erupted, spewing soil and earth in all directions. Luckily for the dumbstruck animals, instead of torrents of molten lava steam and gases, all that came forth was a mole, although, for the watching spectators, considering who it was, was a damn site worse than being smothered in molten lava.

Frozen to the spot, Albert looked in horror as two sets of razor-sharp claws emerged from the mini-eruption, almost skewering him. It was Digger, and, as usual, the first thing he wanted to do on emerging from the molehill was to flatten somebody.

"Alright, who wants some, then?"

A supposed refugee from Australia, the story goes as follows (the way he chooses to tell it, anyway): after a visit to New Zealand, on his way back home, he made the mistake of turning left when he should have gone right, and he had ended up here. Everyone, of course knew that was a bit of a fib, but woe betide anyone who was daft enough to argue the point with him. Very short-sighted when he ventured above ground, he had yet to put in his contact lenses (below ground his short-sightedness didn't matter so much). Until then, he had to identify objects by touch. So, it was reasonable to believe he didn't know that the large over-sized juicy worm he was just about to take a chunk out of was Albert.

Only Albert's angry hiss saved him from a painful bite on the bum.

Not only was the mole very short-sighted, he was also very short-tempered. Despite being only eight inches long, he was afraid of no one; not even Albert. Aggressive by nature, like all his kin, although unlike those who only squabbled among themselves, Digger took on all comers; and the sooner the better as far he was concerned. Owls, weasels, even the hard nut tomcats had yet to get the better of him. Working all day underground had given him powerful forepaws and immensely strong shoulders; he was a match for anyone. Cordial enough when it suited, which, to be honest, was almost never, but watch the sparks fly if anyone rubbed him up the wrong way. No one ever did. Most of Albert's friends were as daft as brushes; absolutely none were suicidal.

Finally putting in his contact lenses, he, at last, recognised his reluctant lunch and apologised, but pointedly not for almost biting Albert in half. "I know I'm late," he explained, "but the underground was busy."

Listening from the pond, Armless blurp, burped. "He always says that."

Unable to understand any of the koi carp's remarks, the mole nevertheless gave her the benefit of his killer look. Armless, though, understood perfectly the mole's unspoken threat, retreating swiftly to the safety of a lily pad. As quietly as she could (she had heard that moles had very good hearing) she blubbled her defiance.

Making sure that the mole's hunger pangs had passed, Albert explained what had happened to Speedy and that Billy was around and looking for trouble, and for him to be careful and to keep his eyes peeled.

The mole wasn't at all impressed with Albert's advice. Looking for trouble was why he had dug himself out of the ground in the first place. "Where is the fluff? I'll sort him out right now."

The mole raised himself on to his hind limbs, claws in a clinch, challenging whoever was daft enough. "C'mon then, if you think you are hard enough! You want some, hey?"

It was exactly the reaction Albert had expected. With Digger, it was par for the course.

*   *   *

The mole watched as K.C. huffed and puffed in his attempt to get everyone ready for his parade. "What's does that stuck up his own backside think he's doing?"

"Who?"

Albert looked over at K.C.

"Oh, you mean, His Royal Poshterior. I don't think he knows."

K.C. was continuing in his futile quest to get every one of the mammals to do as they were told. Needless to say, he was being ignored.

"He's very good, isn't he?" Digger observed.

"Well," Albert explained, "he is the expert."

"Yeah," Digger put in, "and we all know what an 'ex' is."

Albert obliged. "A complete has-been. And a spurt...?"

Both Albert and Digger finished off the old joke loudly, "IS A DRIP UNDER PRESSURE!"

They burst out laughing.

Eventually K.C. managed to get some semblance of order, observing that at least two absentees were not on parade: Speedy, who was still hiding in the sack, and that disgusting frog, Pongo. Pongo, a perfect name for the evil-smelling frog, aptly named by the resident creatures, because, 'Everywhere the frog goes, the pong goes'.

Unseen, Pongo had indeed arrived, his dark blotches, bars and stripes perfect camouflage among the leaves of early spring. He, like all the others, wanted to help Speedy, but was desperate not to be seen. He would have loved to join in the general banter but, sadly, whenever he hopped in to say his hellos, everyone scattered, all crying out, "Argh! Scatter! It's him!"

Whenever the frog was in the area, testing the direction of the wind was second nature for the local wildlife.

The local fauna had also learned very quickly never to amuse him. To make him laugh was to invite disaster. When something struck him as funny, he giggled, causing him to burp. This resulted in the release of foul-smelling, rotten egg breath. That, though, was only the prelude. A full belly laugh, and he farted; the odour so foul and obnoxious that even his fellow amphibians, who were used to living in smelly stagnant ponds, scattered. As small as he was, Pongo's capacity to store wind, and his ability to keep on farting, when any normal animal, large or small, at best, could only manage one or two discharges, was one of the wonders of the animal world.

Even the ever-optimistic Speedy would refuse to tell jokes if the farting frog was in the vicinity. Downwind of the warty cesspool, whenever he was performing could only mean one thing: instant, smelly, eye-watering, lung-burning, desperately calling for your mummy to help, then, finally, rancid limb-twitching paralysis.

Albert watched as K.C. scuttled behind a tree and lifted his leg. Now was his chance to speak to Speedy's friends before the spaniel finished what he was doing.

"Listen in, gang," he hissed.

Immediately, there was a hush.

"Thanks for coming to help. I'm sure there is something we can think of to get Speedy's shell back for him. Once K.C. has stopped buggering about, we'll get our heads together. Okay?"

The crowd murmured in agreement.

"Oh, and one more thing, though. Billy is on the prowl. So, keep your eyes peeled."

There were nods all round.

Frustratingly, K.C. just couldn't stop peeing. He had desperately wanted to urinate on the riff-raff, just to show them who was in charge, and what would happen if they didn't toe the line. Unfortunately, not one of the peasants would stay still long enough to get a good squirt. So, he had to be content with the tree.

Meantime, Speedy, awoken from his slumber by all the barking K.C. had been making, made his way to where everyone had congregated. Albert explained to him what all the fuss was about.

Saying hello, Speedy thanked everyone for coming to help. Some, his gambling friends, were genuinely worried for him. All of them knew of his disastrous dealings with Billy the Bookmaker. Others had turned up to listen to his jokes. With Speedy around, there was never going to be any dull moments.

One who could always be relied upon to have more dull moments than most was the King Charles spaniel. Having finished his wee, he again began barking out his orders. And, although he hadn't found any sign of Pongo, and couldn't be sure whether or not he had turned up, much to the relief of everyone he barked the all-clear anyway, "Frog alert is over."

To his surprise, everyone seemed to be behaving. He decided that now might be as good a time as any to call the rabble to order. He cleared his throat.

"Ahem," he began, "could one have your attention, if you please."

No one was listening to him. Speedy had already gone straight into one of his jokes. "So, she thinks, 'Now we are finally married, I had better tell him about my bad breath'. And he is thinking he had better tell her about his smelly feet. 'Darling', he begins, 'I have something I really must tell you.' She says, 'But, my dearest, there is something I need to tell you also'. He interrupts her, saying, 'I already know what it is you are going to tell me'. She says, 'Oh, and what is that my sweet…?' He says, 'You've been eating my bloody socks again, haven't you?'"

The whole audience erupted in laughter; everyone that is, with the sole exception of the spaniel, who demanded they all put a sock in it. Once more, everyone exploded.

This indiscipline infuriated K.C. Losing his temper, he barked in irritation, "By the Lord Montague's breeches! One cannot hear oneself think anymore!"

Giggling, the crowd waited to see what would happen next.

"Attention, please! You bunch of ill-disciplined rabble!" he barked bad temperedly. "QUIET!"

All the giggling ceased. At long last, it seemed he had his obedience. He was blissfully unaware that it was subterfuge and not subservience that was doing the trick.

"Jolly good show. Now listen in."

He glared at one or two of the creatures who were still chatting.

"Do come on. Let's have you all paying attention now.

No one moved. A reprimand was now the only way, someone he knew he could safely bully. He espied Prof.

"You, sir. Damn you, yes you sir at the back, stand up straight and take that piece of grass out of your beak."

Prof, with only the vaguest idea of where he was, let alone that he had just been told off, continued to stare vacantly at nothing and no one in particular.

The damned insolence of the bird!

With a beatific look on his face, unaware that K.C. was still attempting to get him to obey orders, Prof offered his nearest neighbour, a sparrow, a small slice of his grass cuttings. Foolishly, the smaller bird accepted the wedge, regretting it almost immediately. Mistakenly, instead of chewing, she swallowed. Eyes bulging, wings flapping ineffectively, her tiny claws began beating desperately at her chest. Her friends, having absolutely no sympathy, began to hammer at their own chests, coughing and spluttering in synch with Prof's unfortunate customer.

Prof admonished them all. "If you don't make mistakes, you don't make anything work for you."

At least, they thought he did. Before he could offer any of the others a small taster, K.C. was barking out orders once again.

"Now, can we all recall why we are all here? That is to say, help, Speedy get his shell back?"

This time, everyone stopped messing around and listened to K.C. Perhaps he was about to say something useful; something they could at last understand.

"First things first. Can we corroborate which of you is in attendance and who among you are belated?" he growled. "Let me see now. The frog, damn it! Has anyone seen that damn frog? Does anyone know the whereabouts of that damnable frog?"

"He croaked," Albert called out.

Some of the others began to make very rude farting noises.

Not in the least bit amused, K.C. growled, "Please, could we all have just a little decorum."

Albert laughed again. "Not for me, K.C. I'm a vegetarian."

"I'll have a small piece," called out one of the rabbits. "But only if it's sugar-free."

Not to be left out, Speedy gave his order. "Well K.C., if you are going down to the chippie, I'll have pie and chips. No mushy peas though. They make my farts smell."

This was followed by sounds of pain and even more bogus frog farts.

Desperate to get some order back, K.C. begged, "Please, everyone! Order, damn it! Order everyone! Order! Now!"

"Mine's a pint, landlord," Prof demanded. For a second, he believed he knew where he was.

"Blubble, Burrppp." Armless laughed so hard, she hiccupped and sneezed at the same time, "HICCUBLE, HICCUBLE, ATCHBLUBBLE," causing her pond to froth and boil.

Good-tempered, if only temporarily, Digger laughed and called out, "I'll have what she's been having."

"I wouldn't if I was you," Albert advised. "I've just seen Pongo peeing in the pond."

In the middle of a run-of-the-mill sneeze, stunned, and horrified by Albert's sudden revelation, Armless double 'HICCATCHBLUBBLED'; this time torpedoing herself out of her newly contaminated water desperate to stay above water and to hold her breath for as long as possible. After a few seconds, gravity being the spoilsport it is, tail first, she splashed back into the pond; the cheers of the watching crowd adding to her discomfort.

"Did you see that?" one of the water voles cried in astonishment. "A flying fish!"

"Ah, that's nothing," Tom the old rabbit claimed. "I saw a house fly once and," he lied, "I had a ride on a horsefly last week."

Of course, no one believed a word of it, and he was told to shut up.

*   *   *

Until now, Pongo had been able to restrict himself to a few smiles and smirks. Then he saw his old adversary, Armless, launch herself out of the pond. At long last, he let out a giggle and a burp, followed by an uncontrollable belly laugh. For the first time today he was noticed, or rather his farts were.

His first explosive burp came out with that rotten eggy and stale rotten pondweed smell. All his farts, though, exploded out of his bum with violent intent and, if it had been at all possible, they would have exited his arse with teeth. What was even more underhand: today's farts were silent and came out with socks on. Nevertheless, the stench was still overwhelming.

First to inhale Pongo's lung-burning smelly discharge was a house mouse. "Wow," he coughed, "who dropped that o..." He didn't get to finish the sentence. With tears streaming from bulging eyeballs, he collapsed, in a heap, writhing on the ground; the stink way too much for the mouse's delicate nasal passages.

His neighbour, a shrew, was next to inhale the rancid fetid air; unable to believe what her nose had just sucked up. Perhaps she could turn around and face away from the repellent odour? It didn't make any difference. Whatever it was, it was going nowhere. Not able to take any more, she tried ridding herself of the pollutant by throwing up; the comatose house mouse the unlucky recipient of the deluge. The shrew then attempted to breathe only through her mouth. That didn't help either. In desperation, she tried holding her breath. Nothing she did could rid her of the stench; it was everywhere. And she was only the second victim. From then on, victim after victim went down. No one was immune from the assault. The smell was relentless.

Numerous creatures, all in various stages of distress, began to plead for help, calling for anyone to make it go away. Mums, dads, aunts, uncles. Anyone who could help stop the foul odour from getting up sensitive noses. "Please," they pleaded, "please, make it go away!"

Still, no one knew who had been responsible; who to blame. Although a hedgehog, who just happened to be passing, (coincidentally the same spiny mammal who had earlier in the day helped free two earthworms from worrying about their skin problems, one of them permanently) got some of the blame and was given a good hiding by one of the hares. Others – those who were lucky enough to be further away from the source of the attack and were relatively unharmed – bravely assisted some of the walking wounded to get away. A few of Pongo's previous victims (those who had the misfortune to have encountered this smell before) had a good idea who was responsible, but, without any proof, they could only speculate. A rabbit and a hare, who only moments ago were best friends, now became manic and accused each other of being the source of the smell. Normally an accusation of such magnitude would have ended in fisticuffs. However, because of the lack of breathable air, both thought it wise to continue the argument elsewhere, so they headed for the exit; almost making it. Eyes streaming, hopping first this way and then that, their attempt, like most of the other victims, futile. The repulsive stink, as if impregnated into their fur, followed them everywhere.

It was now only a matter of luck how much of the stench each creature breathed in. No one yet had worked out which was the safest way to run to escape, if indeed there was a safe route.

Tom, the old rabbit who had lied about having ridden a horse fly, was first to locate where the smell was coming from and whose bum was to blame. Unfortunately, he had chosen the wrong direction in which to escape and had slammed head-first into Pongo's reeking backside, collapsing into a heap of useless fur. He was doubly unlucky. As it was the final emission from the frog's backside that did for him. Twitching insanely, he went down, gamely managing to gasp out to the others where the dirty-arsed sod was. It was way too late. Semicomatose creatures, the agonising look on their faces seemingly frozen in tortured grimaces, lay moaning, scattered all over the patio.

However, thanks to Tom's selfless bravery, everyone now knew which area to stay clear of. Luckily for all the tortured souls, a breeze had sprung up, blowing a lot of the stench away, allowing the clean-up to begin. Some, face masks donned, returned to help limping friends. One or two, badly affected by the smell, had to be carried away on makeshift stretchers by their friends. Old Tom, sadly, was now just a gibbering heap of fur and beyond any help.

Pongo had been in smelly heaven though. He had never had so much fun. Even the day he laid low those obnoxious toads wasn't as rewarding as this had been. He would have to do it again sometime.

Albert and one or two of the others, including Speedy, Digger, Prof and K.C, were lucky. None of the frog's reeking emissions had blown their way. All of them shouted out tips and encouragement to the tormented victims; every bit of it useless.

Adding insult to smelly injury, Pongo now hopped on to the almost deserted patio, making the surviving quartet jump. A self-satisfied grin plastered across his face, he enquired, "Am I too late to join in the fun?" Fooling no one and, although he was now empty and had at last stopped farting, he was ordered to stay at a safe distance.

*   *   *

While all the mayhem had been taking place, Digger's normally miserable disposition had temporarily left him, and he had laughed so hard that one of his contact lenses had fallen out. Unable to focus properly, he accidentally barged into Prof. Instantly, his feeling of good humour left him. Squinting hard, he squared up to the dizzy blackbird.

Feather-headed Prof may have been; blind he most certainly wasn't. The wild expression on the mole's face persuaded him to tread very carefully. "Peace, man," he tried.

"Peace off," Digger threatened dangerously.

Ever the optimist, Prof tried once again. "Civility costs nothing, bro."

Digger didn't care how much it cost; he was having none of it. Thumping Prof squarely on the pointed end of his bill, he almost drilled the unfortunate blackbird into the hard ground.

The injured blackbird slowly got back to his feet, reflecting, perhaps a little late in the day, that he had been wrong, and that civility wasn't free after all. It was, he thought, time his laid-back philosophy had a serious overhaul. Still in a bit of a daze, he thought he was hearing things. No, he was right, Digger was having a heated argument with the Mexican gnome. Gnomez, who had heard it all before of course, kept his own council.

Prof agreed with the gnome's reasoning, "You've got the right idea, mate. If you can't fight, wear a big hat."

Chuckling to himself, Albert slid over to where Speedy was sunbathing. "Alright, my old mate? Good here, innit?"

Speedy grinned as the last of the suffering stragglers limped away. "Yeah. Funniest thing since Armless told me she was suffering from hydrophobia."

"I said claustrophobia," the koi carp blubbled defiantly.

"Take a look at K.C.," Albert suggested.

K.C., having had his carefully arranged meeting decimated by that disgusting amphibian, was now bent on retribution. It was about time the bounder was taught a lesson. A jolly good flattening would suffice, now it was safe. Lowering himself on to his belly, he began stalking the now empty frog.

Pongo, still basking in the memory of the havoc he had caused, just missed the dog's first attempt to flatten him, only realising at the last second that he had been the canine's intended target. Paws smacking on the recently vacated ground, the spaniel began chasing after the slippery amphibian. This was fun. His tail wagging madly, he set off once again in hot pursuit. Thwack! "Damn!" he cursed "Almost got the blighter that time!" He was clearly getting better at frog interception.

Pongo decided it would be wise to get out of the dog's firing line, K.C. was getting way too close for comfort. Only just managing to dodge a third attack, he launched himself towards the pond.

Armless, watching from the pond, had been cheering K.C., chastising Pongo every time he escaped the dog's frantic clutches. Suddenly, she realised that the frog was heading back into her pond and, horror of horrors, aiming directly for her.

Panic stricken, and unable to move fast enough, she swallowed much more water than her tiny lungs could hold. Coughing and spluttering out the excess water, 'atchblubbling' in the process, she aquaplaned backwards. In an uncontrolled reverse, she bounced up the small waterfall and into the feeder pond.

Still in mid-flight, Pongo watched the carp reverse out of the pond. Laughing hysterically at the koi's antics, and now unable to control his point of entry, he dive-bombed a string of tadpoles (incidentally the same immature frogs Armless had infected earlier). Away the tiny amphibians flew; some to join Armless in the upper pond; others not so lucky, ending up on the patio. All the surviving youngsters informing the frog exactly what they thought of him. "Bum," they squeaked in unison. "Bum."

Shocked to hear such language from ones so young, Pongo expressed his displeasure, ordering them all not so be rude to their elders. After all, he might well be their dad. Well, he thought, one of them, anyway.

What he wasn't to know was that they weren't swearing at him but had all caught head colds and were calling, "Mum, Mum."

Chapter 13

Seconds after the frog had escaped and decimated the unfortunate tadpoles, K.C. recovered his composure. He would, of course, never admit to enjoying himself; only of exercising his right to rid himself of all unruly and disruptive elements from his meeting. His upper-class snobbish attitude would never have allowed him to admit that he had taken pleasure in the experience. But yes, secretly he had enjoyed the romp while it lasted.

Now though, it was back to the business of the day. But first things first. He would need to give that rabble lazing near Gnomez a piece of his mind, starting with that offensive creature, the mole (small 'm'). He would be well within his rights to have given the snake a thrashing of its lifetime, but the fact that the snake had sharper teeth than him, he sensibly discarded the idea. The unprotected tortoise would, of course, be the easiest to punish, and he did consider it for a moment, but with a shake of his head he discarded that idea too. Bred to be chivalrous, and being of royal stock, he drew the line at being a bully. Stern faced, he trotted up to the group.

"You seemed to be enjoying yourself," Albert greeted him pleasantly.

Careful not to upset Albert, he politely asked if he knew the whereabouts of that impudent serf.

"Which one?"

Albert knew quite a few.

"Are we being deliberately obtuse and obstructive, snake?" K.C. admonished. "The mole, damn you! The mole, what!".

"What?" Albert echoed.

Speedy pretended he hadn't been listening. "What?"

Then, for the first time in its stony life, Gnomez joined in. "What? Who said what?"

Everyone gawped, ready to run at the first sign of movement. To everyone's relief, Digger poked his dirty snout out from behind the gnome.

"Well? Are you lot going to help me look for the lens, or what?"

Immediately the search began. The lens stayed lost.

To lighten the mood, Speedy asked the mole, "Have you considered contacting Mystical Mary to try to get into contact with your missing contact lens?"

Digger's reply, predictably, began and ended with an expletive. With nothing polite in-between.

K.C. was shocked. He had never heard language like it. Well, only the once. When he was a pup he had – accidentally one might add – left a little packet for his master's stockingless feet to find. And the less said about that episode the better. Barking angrily, he yelped his disapproval. "Sir," he admonished the mole, "one does not use that kind of language. Apologise immediately, or brace yourself for a thrashing."

Speedy and Albert looked on in astonishment. Had K.C. lost his marbles, or what? Didn't the spaniel know Digger's reputation for violence?

To the relief of Armless, who had only just managed to get herself back to where she belonged, Pongo leapt out of the pond. Full once again of delicious insects, weeds and, importantly, wind, he sat back to watch the dog fur fly.

"Are you barking at me?" Digger whispered menacingly. He couldn't believe his luck. First, that daft blackbird, now the dog. Brilliant! Two scraps above ground today and it wasn't even teatime. It didn't get much better than this!

"Outside, now!" he demanded.

"You damnable blackguard, Sir!" K.C. yelped. "One is already ensconced externally."

A frown now appeared on Digger's face. "Come here and say that, whatever it was."

Unable to focus too clearly due to his missing lens, and unable to move too far without bumping into things, he waited.

Before K.C. could decide how he could get the better of the mole, Prof, still to completely recover from the earlier thump, unknowingly positioned himself between the protagonists, declaring, "Action speaks louder than words, man."

Digger took him at his word and flattened him for a second time

Tumbling backwards, feathers and beads flying in all directions, the blackbird, with an almighty bump, came to a painful stop. Eventually coming to, he declared, "Wow, bro! That was one awesome trip! Thanks, man."

Eyes crossed, he sank to the ground and was still.

K.C. stared in shock, unable to believe someone that small could pack such a punch. He was beginning to have second thoughts. Perhaps he should have picked on the defenceless tortoise after all, and bugger fair play.

What happened next stopped all thoughts of combat.

*   *   *

Albert had sensed danger, hissing for everyone to stay completely still. The whole group, knowing the snake to be sincere, froze where they stood. Prof, still out cold, was going nowhere.

As ever, even as Pongo had been creating mayhem, Albert had been aware of the possibility of threats from ground level. This menace came from high above. What had probably alerted the raptor from its usual territory to Albert's group was the mayhem and the movement that Pongo's poisonous assault had been responsible for. With the patio now almost empty, Albert's group was the only obvious prey it could target.

It was the only time in any reptile's life it would be unable to defend itself. A snake's worse nightmare. What had first alerted Albert was the shadow that had fleetingly glided across the patio. Perhaps, he had thought, hopefully, the hunter was only passing through? Exposed as they all were, too far away from cover to flee, everybody would have to remain. Scattering now, if the raptor was only on its way to its usual hunting grounds, any movement would certainly have drawn attention to themselves. Unmoving, at least there was a slim chance of it flying past.

It wasn't to be.

The dark shadow once again fell across the patio. It was a peregrine falcon, and its sickle shape could only mean one thing: prey had been selected. The bird, tail and wings closed, already in the stoop, was dropping like a stone and closing in on its quarry. In less than five seconds it would all be over. Sadly, one of them wouldn't be going home for tea.

The raptor was a female; somewhat larger than her male counterpart. Her short neck and broad chest gave her a look of sheer power. Normally, peregrines will only choose birds on the wing and small mammals, but occasionally she would take a snake if they were not alert enough. Her dark eyes were enormous, missing nothing. Any repositioning by the group would have spelt disaster. No one was going anywhere.

Albert and his friends were very much tuned to their own individual survival instincts. Everyone, that is, except the canine. Not understanding the day-to-day logic between prey and predator anymore, K.C., like most domesticated animals, had always been taught to react in a friendly manner. Nevertheless, he understood real fear. So, tail firmly lodged between shaking legs, he remained motionless.

Although it was unlikely that Pongo would have been the raptor's target, he, nevertheless, wished he hadn't been so keen to watch K.C. get his comeuppance and, unlike the spaniel, he understood the trouble he could be in. Of course, it was certain to be him. Ever since he had been a tadpole, misfortune had dogged him. Take earlier, when all he had wanted to do was to help, and, look what happened. Mayhem! He only hoped that if, no, *when* the bird swallowed him, he would be able to fart all the way down its gullet, giving it at the very least bad breath, or, even better than that, chronic indigestion. Saving himself, he knew, couldn't have been easier. All he needed to do was hop back into the pond, swim to the bottom and hide among the weeds. If only he could get his damn legs to work.

Unsurprisingly, Digger was all for sorting the intruder out. Whatever or whoever the hell it was he would give it a bloody good hiding, provided he could see the damn thing to thump it. Unmoving, he readied himself to ambush the unseen interloper.

Swooping ever lower, the falcon accelerated to almost sixty miles an hour, her sharp eyes missing nothing.

Speedy, luckier than the others, had a bodyguard: Gnomez. Grateful that raptors couldn't yet see through cement, he stayed hidden in the shadow of the gnome's huge sombrero. Nevertheless, like the others, he stayed perfectly still.

The falcon, almost at ground level now, claws like giant hooks, closed in on her target: Albert. He, of course, knew from the start that he was the target; the others never were going to be the raptor's choice of food. Although if anyone had made any attempt to move, the falcon would have been on them and would have caused serious injury. Normally, his excellent camouflage would have been enough to save him, but not today. In less than a heartbeat, it would all be over. The falcon would have him and there was nothing he nor, sadly, Digger, could do about it.

Pongo, while unhappy that the bird flew towards Albert, was nevertheless grateful it wasn't to be him.

Albert waited for the fatal blow that would end in darkness.

"OI, YOU! LEAVE MY FRIEND ALONE!"

Incredibly, a millisecond before the falcon gripped Albert, she raised her deadly talons and flew towards the potting shed. In the blink of an eye, the noisy dormouse was clamped in her deadly grip.

Albert thanked his lucky stars that Lonely had called out when he did, distracting the bird from her original target. Why on earth had the tiny rodent put himself in danger like that? But he knew, and was grateful, that the noisy sod had saved his life.

Unknown to the others, the little mouse had deliberately called out. Seeing his best friend in danger, he did the first thing he could think of to help. He had called out. Well, it was for his best pal, wasn't it? Sadly, it seemed, it was also to be for his last pal.

With the heroic dormouse gripped in her deadly talons, and flapping her majestic wings, the falcon soared high into the clear sky.

Lonely, surprisingly still alive, called out, "ALBERT, I WILL ALWAYS–"

Whether it was the shock of hearing an over-loud voice from her supposedly deceased supper, or her grip wasn't as it should have been, the bird lost her grip; the mouse tumbling into the adjacent meadow.

Dozens of disappointed rodents watched as Albert's friend tumbled to safety.

"–LOOOOVE YOUUUUU," Dozy finished, a second before he hit the ground. With nothing more than a sore head, he scampered away before the raptor had the chance to swoop down again.

The sound of happy cheering that had been echoing around the meadow turned, instantly, to jeering immediately the peregrine lost her grip and the dormouse tumbled downwards. Calls of "Useless sodding waste of feathers!" and "My Granny could have done better than you. You berk!" More and more disappointed rodents joined in; all the time the catcalls getting ruder. "You toss wit!" was one, and another advised her to, "Stick your talons where the sun doesn't warm up!" Others were a lot more practical, calling to the raptor to look elsewhere, "No, No, he's over there in the next field, useless git!" Another calling (although the raptor is female), "No, numb pods, not there! Oh, for the love of..." All manner of advice echoed across the meadow; none of it any help.

Lonely was, by now, long gone.

The falcon circled for a few seconds more, then flapped her majestic wings, eventually disappearing over the horizon. But if she hadn't been so angry with herself for dropping Lonely and had circled around once more, she would have seen dozens of tiny titbits, waving at her, all seemingly desperate to be a substitute for her missing lunch.

Speedy emerged from under the sombrero to give Albert one of his 'I'm about to take the mickey' looks. The mouse and Albert in love? Brilliant!

In no mood for levity, Albert warned the naked tortoise, "Take that look off your face or I promise, after what I have just been through, I'll eat you for real this time."

It had been the second traumatic drama of his short life. His mother's violent passing, the previous October, was still a little raw.

Digger grumbled that he never got the chance to tangle with the unseen raptor. Mumbling his disappointment, he set off in another fruitless attempt to find his missing lens.

K.C., not really understanding the nature of how things were in the very dangerous world Albert and his friends lived in, was still determined to put his royal paw forward and carry on. "Ahem, snake," he growled. "One really ought not to disremember the purpose of this gathering, that I, and I alone, snake, went to a lot of time and trouble organising, what? Damned incompetent and inconvenient, if you were to ask me."

What? Didn't the toffee-nosed prat not see what had almost happened to me? I could well have been bird food! He hissed angrily, "Listen, you royal pain in the bum! Do you not see? Everyone, except us five, has buggered off. And, will you, for once in your life, speak in a language I, all of us, can understand. English will do, if you can manage it!"

K.C. was incensed that Albert could say such a thing. That he, a Montgomery Smythe, was being accused of not conversing in English. Kings and Queens English, damn it! "How dare you, sir! One does engage in 'English'. Courteously and with decorum and pellucidity."

Understandably, Albert wasn't quick enough to react.

"Now, reference the missing carapace, snake. Remember? Really, I don't know why I bother sometimes, I really don't."

Albert, as usual, whenever K.C. was in full flow, was lost.

"The assignment, snake. What does one propose to do to rectify the conundrum, eh?"

He waited in vain for Albert's reply.

"For goodness sake, snake, will you get a grip? The missing shell. How does one propose to regain the carapace? I'm far too good for these peasants," he muttered to himself, "far too good."

"All right then, smart-arse," Albert retorted, eventually getting K.C.'s point. "You're so clever, you tell me."

Before K.C. could respond, the koi carp, who had overheard Albert's conversation with the hare, put forward an idea no one could understand, pre-empting K.C.'s suggestion, which, in all probability, no one would understand. "Why don't we all sneak round and take it while Billy's still having his lunch? The bookmaker won't be expecting that, and we know where to go now, don't we?"

Without holding out much hope, Albert asked the group if anyone had any idea what the hell she was blubbling about.

"I do," volunteered Pongo, making everyone jump. Just in case of accidents, the wind direction was carefully checked. The frog sighed sadly, reluctantly interpreting his arch opponent's watery proposal.

Albert was impressed, "That's a good idea," he declared. "Never thought of that one. Well done, Armless."

The koi carp puffed out her multi-coloured chest, blubbled her thanks and gave the frog a self-satisfied smirk.

Still upset that he hadn't got to tangle with the falcon, Digger grumbled that he hadn't thought of it because it was "too bloody obvious."

Speedy who was a veteran when it came to contact with the bookmaker, said "too bloody dangerous."

"Nothing ventured, nothing gained, man," Prof twittered from the safety of his new perch high on the Mexican's sombrero, well away from the threat of more violence from Digger. If he remembered rightly, moles couldn't climb, so he was safe. He hoped. Having only just recovered from the earlier unwarranted assaults, he wasn't about to go for the hat-trick. His idea of cool did not include getting regular deliveries of mole knuckles. Laid back he may well have been, laid out just wasn't part of the deal. No, up here will do for now, thank you.

Almost causing Prof to lose his balance, Digger agreed, shouting out, "The soppy bird's right. What are we waiting for? Let's go!"

Albert suggested they first devised a plan. "What we need to do is work out how to get close to Billy's without being seen, how to get Speedy's shell away from him and his bodyguards and, most importantly, how not to get seven kinds of crap beaten out of everyone."

Not immediately getting his own way, Digger glared menacingly at nothing and no one in particular, his unfocused lens-less left eye, to the relief of everyone except Prof, eventually settling on Gnomez. "Tell me the plan!" he demanded. "Quick, before I punch your lights out!" Not getting an answer, only a startled squawk from the terrified bird, his one good eye eventually settled on K.C. The terrified spaniel scampered behind Albert, wondering why the mole seemed to take great delight in beating up his friends. Almost on the wrong end of a good hiding earlier, he had no intention of getting close enough to ask.

"Right." Albert, having worked out a plan, beckoned everyone closer. "First we'll need air cover, lots of it. Prof, this is where you come in."

"Cometh the hour," the blackbird quoted proudly, "cometh the bird, man."

Albert glared menacingly; he'd had just about enough of Prof's quiz words.

"Eek! What?" the blackbird screeched in panic. He had seen that look before (it was he who had whitewashed Albert's head earlier in the day), and, if he remembered correctly, snakes could climb. Normally, for a sane bird, flying its way out of trouble would have been easy. The difficulty for Prof would be working out which way was up. Flattened twice by that punch-drunk mole hadn't been the nicest things that had happened to him already today; getting intimate with Albert's tonsils would certainly be counted as one of the worst. He thought it best to placate the snake. "Hey, peace, bro. No problem. Anything I can do to help, Albert, just ask."

Chapter 14

Albert surveyed the tiny group. Out of the whole group, Digger would be the only one who could be relied on in a scrap, so long as he was able to see who he was thumping. Not that he would care. Friend or foe, it was all the same to him. K.C. wouldn't be much use in a scrap, and as for the blackbird, he sighed sadly. Although, to be fair, at least K.C. and Prof were willing. And Speedy, perhaps he could tell jokes until they laughed themselves into submission.

Having explained most of his plan to the others, he wished them all good luck.

"Tis a far better thing I do…" Prof began, before getting a very cross, cross-eyed look from Digger, instantly shutting him up.

Feeling terribly left out, Armless popped her head out of the pond. "What would you like me to do?" she blubbled. It was after all her idea in the first place. Pongo relayed her desperate plea.

In no mood for small talk, Digger once again gave the koi his killer look and cruelly informed her, "You can be the fish supper."

"Get knotted, you over-stuffed furball!" she retorted.

Understanding her attitude, if not her language, Digger ordered Pongo to translate.

Not wishing to get involved in an argument between a psychopath and a suicidal fish, Pongo hopped back into the pond. Getting a little of his own back in retaliation for the encouragement she had been giving K.C. earlier, he informed Armless, "Do you have a death wish, or what? Don't you know moles are bloody good underwater swimmers?"

Unsure whether or not the frog was telling her the truth, she retreated, hiding behind the remaining string of frog spawn. Desperate to get their own back in return for the colds she had given them earlier, the surviving aquatic larvae began calling out to the mole, "Oi, you, she's hiding over here! Hurry up before she wipes her nose on us again."

Albert was having difficulties trying to work out how to transport Speedy to where he knew Billy was. Despite his name and reputation, with or without the shell, and with the five o'clock deadline fast approaching, it was going to take Speedy much too long on foot. Albert had to admit, he was stumped. Unfortunately, he was going to have to bite the bullet and ask K.C. He wouldn't understand a word, of course, but, anyway, here goes.

"Erm, K.C.," he began, "any thoughts on how we can transport Speedy to Billy's? Obviously walking there will be too slow for him. Any ideas?"

He held his breath.

The spaniel, delighted to be asked, puffed out his royal chest in importance. "Procrastinate for not another instance, dear boy. One shall reappear forthwith with a suitable conveyance to transfer the tortoise."

Albert had been quite right. He hadn't understood a bloody word.

In no time at all, K.C. had returned carrying a frisbee, attached to which was a length of twine. Tail wagging, he dropped the plastic disc next to Albert.

This was too much for Albert. "You want to play?" He was furious.

Steady, old chap! One must remember, one is dealing with under stairs riffraff. "Observe."

Knowing how slow peasants are to take even the simplest of instructions, he painstakingly, step by step, explained how to transport Speedy. Frustratingly, as he had expected, nobody was any the wiser. Trying again, he flipped the frisbee over, revealing the inverted underside.

"Suitably capacious and convenient in which the tortoise can be suitably conveyed, what?"

K.C. stared at three blank faces. Four, if you counted Prof. Before he could stop himself, he barked angrily, "It's for the damnable tortoise to be ferried in, you moronic cretins!"

Luckily, for him, no one seemed to know what a cretin or a moron was. His idea, though, was getting almost universal approval.

Albert was impressed and said so. "Excellent idea, K.C. Well done."

"Credit where credit's due, man," Prof declared, caught up in Albert's enthusiasm, having only a slight idea of what was going on.

Never one to give credit, due or otherwise, Digger demanded a trial run. Ordering the tortoise to get on to the plastic frisbee if he knew what was good for him, he demanded K.C. to begin pulling immediately. Without further ado, the spaniel clamped the twine between his teeth and set off slowly around the patio.

At first, Speedy was grimly hanging on, not liking the experience one bit. After a while, though, he began to relax; he was beginning to enjoy the experience. This was much easier than he had imagined. Calling to the spaniel, he ordered him to accelerate. K.C. immediately increased his speed from a sedate trot to a mad gallop. The faster the spaniel accelerated, the more excited Speedy became. Full of confidence now, he stood and waved to his astonished friends.

Albert encouraged the spaniel to go even faster, calling him to, "GO, GO!"

Mishearing the command, believing that Albert had called, "Whoa, whoa!" K.C. came to a sudden halt. However, the frisbee continued on its journey; the spaniel as surprised as everyone to see the tortoise go hurtling past. He hadn't thought about how to stop the damn thing. Still, one couldn't think of everything, could one?

"Where's the brakes?" Speedy screamed. "How do you stop the bloody thing?"

One short second after K.C. halted (the twine still held firmly in his teeth), the frisbee did the same. He had, after all, thought of everything. (Well, almost everything).

Catapulted off the stationary frisbee, cartwheeling and spinning, arms and legs akimbo, neck and exposed vegetables outstretched, Speedy pirouetted and disappeared into the overlong long grass.

"Bloody show-off!" Albert called out after the disappearing tortoise.

A minute later, none the worse following his acrobatics, Speedy made his way back on to the stationary frisbee, claiming he wanted to do it all over again. "Outstanding!" he announced, jumping back on to the sled. "The Ritz, my man!" he excitedly ordered K.C. "And don't spare the dogs!"

Tail wagging, trying not to grin, K.C. picked up the cord between his teeth and awaited the word to go. This was going to be fun.

Albert pointed to a rarely used pathway, overgrown with weeds and early spring flowers. "I think the best way is to go through the woods. Yeah, definitely, through the woods, I think."

K.C., was determined to have the last word. After all, who was leader of this rabble anyway? "Designate one's thoughts to the job in hand, snake. One has got other appointments today, don't you know?" With that, he sniffed, picked up the tow rope and trotted away.

Albert, turned to the mole. "Digger, follow them and keep your eyes focused."

Only after he had been given the sourest of looks did he realise his unfortunate choice of words. Digger, sadly, was still minus his left contact lens, mumbling darkly to himself, complaining he could only just look where he was going, never mind look after an excuse for a dog. Nevertheless, he chased after his charges. He had, in fact, discovered that, if he fluttered his unfocused left eye, while at the same time opening and closing his right in a sequence of, left, right, blink, flutter, flutter, blink – but it had to be in that exact sequence; otherwise he veered to his left after every other step – a little unsteadily at first, he began to gain ground on Speedy and the spaniel.

Surprising him, the closer he got to the pair, the quicker K.C. accelerated away from him. Is the mole coming on to him? Why does the bounder keep winking at me? Has the peasant taken an unhealthy liking to me? He became even quicker in his attempt to extend the gap between himself and his, unwelcome, admirer. Only when Speedy was catapulted into a clump of stinging nettles did the mad cycle of blinks, winks and sprints cease.

Panting, Digger tried to explain his predicament.

Not one hundred per cent satisfied that the mole's explanation was completely to his liking, but not wanting to get the promised thumping, K.C. slowed down. It was still rather disconcerting to see Digger winking at him every time he happened to glance in the mole's direction.

With Speedy back on board, the trio set off once more; this time, much to the relief of K.C., with Digger in the lead. Speedy, oblivious to the spaniel's misgivings, continued to tug on the stinging nettles. Fifty yards further on, the increasingly nervy dog stopped for a pee.

Silently, the frisbee slid to a halt directly under the spaniel's belly button. Unaware he was about to get a good soaking, Speedy continued removing the stings. Fortunately for him, K.C. couldn't see him, so, as usual unable to decide on a suitable target, he decided he could wait, and set off once more.

Apart from one small detour, the trio continued making good progress, although there was still no sign of Albert. Digger had by now got used to his affliction, enabling him to travel in a reasonably straight line, only once having to lean on the panicky spaniel to get him going in the right direction again. K.C., still to be convinced the contact and winks were due to any missing lens, kept his distance.

Then, having got this far, with only one or two minor arguments and without any mishaps, they were disappointed to find a small river barring any further progress.

Sensibly, they would wait until Albert arrived.

*   *   *

Back at the fishpond, Albert was shedding scales, desperately trying to explain the first part of his plan and Prof's vital role in it. The bird-brained blackbird, from the safety of his new perch high on the gnome's sombrero, enquired, once again, "Sorry, Albert, what was it you want me to do?"

Albert, patiently, explained the whole scheme again. This time, he was rewarded with an encouraging, "Birds of a feather flock together, man."

"Off you go then," his patience, at last, rewarded.

"And why would I want to do that?" Prof replied with equal patience; Albert's instructions already forgotten. Although, if he – Prof – remembered correctly, it had something to do with him gathering... No, it's gone again. The withering look he got from Albert helped a little. He leapt from the gnome's sombrero, desperately trying to remember two things at once. Albert's complicated instructions and, and...what was it? He immediately crash-landed, having forgotten to flap his wings. Brushing himself down, he apologised. "It's always the first step that is difficult, Albert."

Would he like a push?

Declining Albert's offer, images of the snake hanging from his backside was incentive enough. With untidy feathers and beads flapping disjointedly, he was at last airborne.

Albert watched Prof weave his way skywards, hoping against hope the blackbird remembered his instructions. He had one last piece of his plan to put into place, then he would join the others. A minute later and he was on his way. Slithering through the overlong grass, it wasn't long before he had caught up with his bickering friends.

"Raft?" Digger was saying to Speedy. "Next, you'll be suggesting we wait for the local ferry to come along so we can thumb a lift. Soppy git."

He winked at K.C., who back-pedalled a safe distance. The mole, of course, believed burrowing under the river the best course of action.

Albert immediately grasped what the problem was. "There is an easier way," he informed them.

Digger was convinced that tunnelling was the best option; a reasonable argument if you happened to dig for a living. "All right then, know-all. How?"

"Well, we could use that bridge."

Stung that he hadn't noticed the bridge, K.C. gave an embarrassed cough. "Ahem, snake, I already knew that."

Digger, head popping up from under a mound of dirt, muttered an even weaker repost. "I had already started digging."

Confident that he had got one over on the spaniel, Albert set off for the bridge. The others swiftly followed, though not before Digger had given K.C. the most withering of looks, putting the blame squarely on the canine for not seeing the bridge in the first place and embarrassing him. Winking once again, he happened to look across to the frisbee where Speedy was sitting. Believing that the mole had been teasing K.C., he winked back. Worryingly for Speedy, Digger continued to wink and blink at him, as if conveying a secret message meant only for him. Becoming increasingly embarrassed, he turned away. The sooner he got his shell back, the safer and more comfortable he would feel. Must be a very lonely life though, having to live and work underground all the time, suddenly feeling sorry for the mole. Abruptly changing his mind when the mole fluttered his eyes at him again.

Digger was wishing he could see properly again. That bloody tortoise seems to think I fancy him! Even that excuse for a dog thinks I've got the hots for him. Some so-and-so's going to kop it shortly. Friend or foe, I don't much care which. He looked up to see what that snotty snake was up to. Getting his blinks and his winks mixed up, he only just managed to waddle up to Albert, who he thought was tired and was resting near a couple of fallen branches. Striking up a conversation, he enquired if the snake was okay. He groaned in frustration when Albert returned from examining the bridge to ask him what the bloody hell he thought he was doing talking to a dead tree?

Returning once again to the bridge, Albert cautiously tested the far side of the bridge for dangerous alien vibrations. There were, of course, the usual array of small mammals but, forked tongue crossed, no real dangers. Not yet, anyway.

Almost eighty years old, the bridge was on the verge of collapse; the wooden structure riddled with rot, seemingly held together by vine, most of which had entwined itself around what remained of the broken handrail. Albert hoped the rotten timbers would bear the weight of himself and the others long enough for the two journeys they were going to have to make.

Still quarrelling, his friends arrived, Digger still having a go at K.C.

What no one except Speedy had known, not twenty yards from the patio was a ford used by all the animals whenever they journeyed back and forth to place their bets with the bookmaker. He could have told his friends earlier but, not wishing to spoil the fun he was having, he conveniently forgot to mention the easier option to the others.

Albert was explaining to the group that on no account must there be more than one of them on the bridge at any one time. It was just too unstable. "Understand?" They did. He also insisted everyone be as quiet as they possibly could. Silence from now on was imperative, so close were they to where he had been told by the hare that Billy was likely to be.

First to cross the creaking bridge was Albert; again testing the air for danger. Satisfied that all was clear, he was followed by a very pumped-up mole, just aching to fill someone in. Next to cross was K.C., and the only thing he was aching to do was pee. He knew he should have gone earlier when he had the chance.

Albert was still a little on edge, but so far everything seemed to be going well. Maybe they would be lucky and get away without too many mishaps. Hopefully, Digger behaved himself and only punched someone when it was necessary and Prof remembered what he had to do. "Quietly does it," he insisted. He was beginning to feel rather proud of his little troupe. He looked towards K.C., who had just reached the centre of the bridge. With himself and Digger across, the spaniel almost over the bridge and still no one had made any untoward noise. Satisfied, he turned to slide away.

Unfortunately, he hadn't counted on the spaniel's overactive bladder.

Two thirds of the way across the bridge, K.C. could wait no longer. Cocking his leg, he took careful aim, intending to saturate one of the uprights. Missing by a good foot, he squirted the pressurised liquid directly into the stream below, the noise almost causing the others to empty their own bladders.

Off the bridge, Albert complained, "Couldn't you be a little louder? I'm not sure everyone in the meadow got the message."

Shamefaced, K.C., unable to stem the flow, apologised; the ear-splitting din making them all cringe as the water below the bridge fizzed and bubbled.

"Sorry, old boy. One just couldn't wait."

Albert begged him to hurry up; desperate to get him off the bridge as quickly as possible.

"Can I thump him, Albert? He deserves it," Digger asked, desperate to belt someone – anyone – and the sooner the better as far as he was concerned.

"Tempting," Albert agreed. "Best wait. Maybe later," he promised. Signalling the still-urinating canine, he urged him to get on with it.

As soon as Speedy had crossed and they were well away from the bridge, Albert directed them into the thick vegetation, insisting that everyone kept their eyes and ears open, or, in

Digger's case, his one good one, and no noise. He looked directly at K.C.

Almost immediately, they could hear noises coming from the other side of the thicket. "Billy?" Speedy whispered.

Needing to get a closer look, Albert explained what he intended to do. And, until he had confirmed that Speedy was right and it was indeed Billy, he suggested they stay hidden. Silently, he slid through the thick hedgerow; the only barrier now separating friend from foe. Albert slipped silently through the thick undergrowth. Forked tongue flicking from side to side, he immediately detected danger. Yes. It was Billy.

Chapter 15

Billy, Billy the Bookmaker or, as the local sheep farmers had named him, Billy the Hat, is a black-faced Swaledale sheep. A ram. He had been sold, or rather, his pregnant mother had, and transported from the Pennines to where he now called home. Billy, like all his breed, had horns. However, unlike all the other rams on this rather isolated sheep farm, he was instantly recognisable. He was the only sheep wearing a hat. A trilby. Hence the obvious nickname.

Despite his violent reputation, and the rumours of how he had, as a lamb, seen off herds of angry foxes, etc., Billy's upbringing was a little less violent and a lot more traumatic. Born a twin, he was immediately abandoned by his mother. The ewe, not having enough milk to feed two, instinctively chose the lamb she believed the strongest, sadly leaving Billy to get on with it and take his chances with the local predators. Rather than use his heroics in saving the flock, he was himself plucked to safety by the farmhands, always on the lookout for abandoned youngsters at this time of year.

He would be weaned in the farmhouse and, only when he was big and strong enough to fend for himself, was he to be allowed out. Sadly, while still being looked after by the sheep farmer's daughter, the foot and mouth epidemic struck. The cull that followed, not distinguishing between animals who had the disease and those lucky enough to be immune, was brutal. Out of the whole flock of newly purchased sheep, including

Billy's mother and his sister, he was the sole survivor. Sensibly, he was kept isolated from the outside world and only when the all-clear had been given, would he be allowed out.

On a cold November day, he was at last to be freed. Ordered by the farmer to get out of the farmhouse, do what he was bought for and to start earning his keep, the puzzled ram was then unceremoniously booted into the farmyard. There, waiting in the sheep pen, presumably for him, stood line upon line of the farmer's newly purchased flock of impatient ewes; all desperate to be first in line and get a good look at the handsome ram.

For a few seconds, he stood open-mouthed, wondering what the heck was going on. Bleating loudly, the ewes began calling for him to get on with it. Could he not see, they were freezing their teats off in this weather? Billy, unlike Albert, knew exactly what was expected of him and immediately started to earn his keep. The farmer, a veteran who had seen it all before, watched for a while, just to make sure that the ram got the hang of things and wasn't making too much of a hash of it. Satisfied everything was in working order, he went home for his breakfast.

Billy watched the sheep farmer disappear back into the farmhouse. More confident now, he began headbutting the older ewes away. One or two, those who had already been serviced, tried pushing their way back into the queue, claiming they had been promised preferential treatment and had every right to go back for seconds. Rightly, given the raspberry, they were all unceremoniously bundled away, promised a good hiding and told to bugger off and not come back.

*   *   *

Spring arrived, and with it came lambing season. All around the neighbouring sheep farms could be heard the joyful bleating of new-born lambs. Sadly though, not on Billy's side of the fence. No matter what the farmhands did to persuade the seemingly expectant mothers to part with their offspring, nothing happened. The shepherds waited and waited, as anxious as the ewes were. It soon became clear though that something was very badly amiss. Not one of the ewes gave birth to anything resembling a lamb. Billy, quite obviously, had not done his job as well as everyone on the farm had assumed.

The farmer was furious and was all for giving Billy the chop. It was only due to the intervention of the sheep farmer's daughter that prevented Billy from ending up on the dinner table. He was, however, banned from the sheep pens and warned never to show his useless face around the farm. Before exile was imposed, however, the farmer tied his old trilby to Billy's curly horns, making him instantly recognisable. It would give the disappointed farmhands the greatest of pleasure whenever they crossed the ram's path to give him a bloody good kick up the backside. Useless so-and-so.

The ewes, understandably, were as upset as the sheep farmer and lined up to hurl hurtful insults. "There he is," the ewes would bleat, "Billy, the blank sheep of the farmyard!"

and, "Watch out girls, here he comes! The Sherriff of Nothingham!"

Getting his own back, he convinced the whole flock that he had seen the farmer with a shotgun. Apparently, he said, all the ewes had caught the ovine viral disease, scrapie, and he was looking to cull the lot of them. Laughing, he watched the whole soppy lot of them stampede for the sheep dip. I'll bet, he sniggered, none of the silly sods pushed their way back into the queue for seconds this time!

The farmhands only ever caught Billy for his promised kicking a few times, and he promised himself after perhaps his third and worst booting that it would be the last. From then on, he was always one step ahead of the shepherds, vowing, from now on, that he would get his retaliations in first. Not against the shepherds, obviously, but with any creature who crossed him.

Not long after his exile, he met up with the pair who were soon to become his minders: Knuckles, who was a particularly nasty bulldog, and Nipper, a Jack Russell terrier. Both, like himself, were in disgrace, although for entirely different reasons. The pair were on the run after vicious assaults on any number of postmen and other attacks on the local milkmen. There may have been others, but, up until now, these were only 'alleged' teeth marks.

On his short time on the farm, Billy had watched how most animals loved to bet among themselves. But no one had thought about taking the gambling too seriously. He was going to change all that. He began by taking small wagers. First, from the farm animals, and later, larger and larger bets from creatures of the meadow, and, if that worked out, he would set up a betting shop in the disused barn in the far corner of the meadow. He would of course need protection, to make certain that his winnings would be safe. And with Knuckles and Nipper on the payroll, no one would dare renege on lost bets, knowing the good hiding they would be in for if the debt wasn't paid up.

His betting empire quickly grew and, as he discovered, the more the creatures lost, the more they would gamble. It was money for old wool.

*   *   *

Albert had seen all he needed to see. The ram and his friends were far enough away from the hedgerow not to interfere with what he had in mind. And he could see Speedy's shell, which, luckily, wasn't being guarded, and which wasn't that far away from the hedge where he and his friends had camped. He was in the process of making his way back unseen and unheard, slithering silently, when an almighty crash on his side of the hedge made all thoughts of stealth superfluous. Prof had made his usual hash of landing.

Albert arrived back just as Digger was helping the dizzy blackbird back to his feet. Fearing the worst, he assumed the mole had belted the bird, or, hopefully, he was only helping the bird to stand up straight. Either way, Prof, fresh grass cutting clamped in his beak, wouldn't remember whether his inept landing was just a bad trip or if indeed the mole had lamped him one. Again. Before Albert could ask, he was told, "No, I haven't, but let's face it, there's still plenty of time."

Albert moved Prof out of range. "Everything set, Prof?" he enquired.

"Attack is the best form of defence, man," the blackbird quoted confidently.

He assumed that had been a yes.

Turning to K.C., Albert gave him his instructions. "Right, when I give the signal, I want you to move as close as you can to the hedge. Okay?"

"Affirmative, snake."

Keeping watch, if that is all one needed to do to keep the peasant happy, fine. He still had his doubts that someone of his standing and position should be this close to the front line, even with that damn mole on his side. (One good thing, at least it had stopped winking at everyone.) It was all very well organising this escapade from the safety of base camp, but, being this adjacent to the fighting clearly wasn't necessary or indeed suitable for officers of his rank.

Albert interrupted his train of thought. "Are you listening?"

K.C. wasn't, but he gave a nervous nod anyway.

"Right. Once Prof has done his thing, I want you through the hedge as quickly as possible, grab Speedy's shell," Albert explained exactly where he could find it, "then back here as quickly as possible. Got that?"

Once more, the spaniel nodded absently.

"And please," he insisted, "don't stop for a pee."

Damn cheek, telling a fellow when one can and cannot relieve oneself! Who does he think he is, anyway? Funnily enough, he was desperate to go again. He wondered if now would be a good time to pee all over the snake, show it who's boss. Then again, perhaps he would wait until a more opportune time presented itself. He should never have allowed the snake to take over command of his squad in the first place. If he had had his way, they would be negotiating with Billy, suspending any future hostilities, even paying a ransom for the return of that damnable shell. Anything but fisticuffs. He was getting extremely nervous.

He wasn't the only one getting edgy. Albert was experiencing the same emotion, but for entirely different reasons. What was worrying Albert was the fact that, so far, everything seemed to be going too well. He gave Digger his final instructions. "When K.C. returns with Speedy's shell, I want you to take care of him, right?"

Winding Albert up, Digger gave him an evil grin. "It'll be my pleasure."

"No, not him, you idiot! Anyone who happens to be following him."

Suffering spitballs, where's my aspirin? Better get started then, before Digger forgets whose side he's supposed to be on.

"Ready, lads?"

Nods all round.

"Right. Give the signal, Prof."

"Signal, Albert? Signal?" The bird, still with a piece of fresh-cut grass in his beak, stared vacantly at Albert. Albert pretended to bite him, frightening the bird into emitting a panicked cry. "Pink, pink, pink." That was the supposed battle cry, which, hopefully, would begin the first stage of Albert's master plan.

Nothing happened.

K.C. looked triumphantly at Albert and harrumphed. Digger gave Albert an unfocused one-eyed pitying look. Albert glared at the blackbird. "Digger, remind him why he's here." Which immediately focused Prof, persuading him to try just that bit harder.

"It's cool, man," he assured Albert. "Practice does make perfect."

The second time, Prof got the squawk just right.

"PINK, PINK, PINK!"

A few second later, the sky turned black. Birds of all shapes and sizes swooped out of the trees in their dozens. Crows and rooks flew together, with sparrows and robins doubling up. Even magpies and starlings joined in. Blackbirds had also volunteered, outnumbering them all. Normally, the different species of bird would never socialise. But, just this once, thanks to an insane blackbird, they all wanted the same. That was: to create mayhem.

The whole group watched in awe as the birds circled overhead. Prof, Albert thought proudly, had certainly exceeded himself. Perhaps he wasn't as daft as he pretended to be. So far, so good.

No one moved; perversely all wishing to be near when the carnage began.

It took less than a second for it all to go horribly wrong.

Realising too late who the targets were to be, the expressions changed from ecstatic delight to the hideous realisation of what they were in for. As requested by Prof, the birds were to attack everything and anything that moved, regardless of what they might hear from the victims. Unfortunately, and unsurprisingly, he had got his descriptions mixed up. As described, Albert and his crew were now perceived as the enemy, so, it was on Albert and his allies that the carnage began.

The birds held nothing back. Beaks bit and pecked, claws scratched and gouged, and wings beat at anything or anyone who moved. No one escaped the assault, and Digger got the worst of it. The blackbirds, all of whom had earlier witnessed Prof get his thumping, were on a totally different agenda to the rest of the flock and had already decided that the mole needed to be taught a lesson and get his comeuppance. Dozens of the songbirds, normally the most placid of feathered vertebrates, squawked and screamed in their excitement, taking it in turns to cause as much pain as they could on the mole. Unable to see who to whack first, Digger was mercilessly bitten, scratched and set upon, time and time again.

Just when it seemed that the worst was over for everyone and the birds had got their money's worth, a second wave of birds took over. Eventually, mercifully, this second wave tired and flew back into the trees, all of them singing joyfully, congratulating themselves on a job well done.

Bloodied and bruised, Albert, Digger and K.C. advanced on the untouched blackbird. Astonishingly, even with the furious trio advancing on him, Prof seemed unconcerned; more interested in covering himself with dead foliage than getting a good hiding.

"No need to do that. We'll bury you ourselves," Digger promised.

It quickly became obvious why Prof was building a shelter. The bombers had arrived.

A full squadron of pigeons was swooping out of the sky. Big, fat, obese – and most of them incontinent – they came in low; all with full loads and bomb doors already open. No one escaped from the downpour of poo. Asked by Prof to crap on anything that moved, they did so, as was usual for the pigeons, with enthusiasm and gay abandon. Pooing on whoever they took a fancy to; second nature to the overweight flying toilets.

Thirty seconds later and it was all over. Prof was quickly out of his makeshift shelter and knew exactly what would happen next if he didn't get the hell out of there, sensibly exiting. For the first and probably the last time in his dizzy life, he found flight no problem.

Albert, blooded, bleeding and covered in bird muck, saw the mess Digger was in, poo dripping off his nose, and began to laugh. "What do you reckon, Digger?"

"Well," the mole, in a worse state than Albert, hazarded a guess, "it ain't icing sugar."

"No, old boy," the spaniel, his fur matted with blood and poo, for once in his life immediately got in on the joke. "It isn't clotted cream either."

Even though all three were scratched, bleeding, in pain and smelling to high heaven, they burst out laughing. "Ssh," Albert warned, trying and failing to stifle his laughter, "or they will hear us."

It was too late; they already had. Knuckles had put his head through the gap in the hedgerow, curious to know what all the noise was about, and what was that smell?

Albert whispered to the spaniel, "Get him, K.C."

"What?" K.C. was incredulous. "Me?" He wanted to know if Albert was mad. "Are you insane, sir? That happens to be a bulldog."

"At least do something," Albert suggested. "Bark at the damn thing."

"Grr," was all the spaniel could manage.

"What? Grr? I can bloody grr! Bark, man! Bark!"

Desperate not to upset the owners of so many teeth, Albert's included, he tried again. "Bark, bark." Even to him that sounded feeble.

Knuckles, unable to fathom out what on earth these dung-coloured smelly apparitions could be, barked out a good-natured and friendly hello. "BARK, BARK."

On hearing the bulldog's loud greeting, Digger whispered, "Point me in the right direction, Albert."

The unsuspecting canine grinned as the ghostly apparition waddled towards him. What was it? And why the hell did it keep winking at him?

His target now in focus, Digger fluttered his eyes once more, then wiped the smile from the face of the bulldog.

"Dow!" Knuckles yelped. "By dose! You've broken by dose!" Just in time, he pulled his head back, escaping a second haymaker.

The birds were back again. Instinctively everyone ducked. This time, much to the relief of Albert and the others, they were overshooting the hedgerow to, hopefully, give Billy and his friends as good a seeing-to as Albert and the others had been given. And, by the sounds coming from the bookmaker and his chums, they were.

Sadly, the assault, this time, had to do without any bomber cover. Waiting in the trees to go again, the pigeons willing and still red in the face from their earlier efforts hadn't had the time to reload and, no matter how hard they squeezed, the only discharge was a pathetic 'Phsstt', and even that little squirt didn't smell. But, to be fair, they did join in the assault on Billy and his two compatriots.

Grateful to be given a second chance, Albert informed K.C. that now would be a good time to go and get Speedy's shell.

But K.C. was going nowhere. Covered in bird droppings, bitten, scratched and barked at by an angry bulldog – even angrier now that it had had its nose broken – there was absolutely no way he was going into harm's way and one was taking no more orders from that damn snake. Absolutely no way. Never. He sniffed, looking defiantly towards Albert.

His friends had other ideas. Digger advanced towards him from one direction, Albert from another; one to bite him and the other, probably, to knock the living fur out of him.

Thinking very quickly about what was about happen, it didn't take long for K.C. to change his mind. Perhaps he might help after all. But just this once, mind you.

Yelping, and with his tail tucked firmly between his legs, he scrambled through the hedgerow. The terrified spaniel emerged from the greenery; instantly ready to surrender, or be chased and eventually savaged by a very angry bulldog. Neither scenario happened. Instead, chaos greeted him. The birds, having quickly got their enthusiasm for violence back, continued where they had earlier left off, pecking and gouging once again and, if it were possible, to make up for their earlier error with even more vigour.

Unused to being on the wrong end of a good hiding, Billy was bleating for the birds to stop. Nipper's whining was not helping, and poor Knuckles was pleading for the birds to, "Please, da dose! Keep away from da dose!"

Meanwhile, K.C. spotted the shell and nervously scampered across to pick the damn thing up. It was safe. Understandably, no one had the slightest interest in stopping the smelly ghost-like apparition from retrieving the abandoned shell; each individual under attack had their own problems to deal with. Clamping the shell between chattering teeth, K.C. got the hell out of there.

Albert was getting the mole ready. "Okay, Digger. Keep your eyes, sorry, your eye, peeled, and if anyone comes through the hedge, flatten 'em. Anyone, okay?"

What Albert should have added was anyone but K.C.

"It's about time too!"

After two aborted attempts, Albert guided Digger to the hole in the hedgerow; the point where the spaniel was likely to reappear. Digger was much happier now the snake had given him a legitimate target to go for. It was all very well giving your pals a friendly tap now and again, but that didn't count as real violence. Sharing his pastime with his friends, when his shift was over, was an ideal way to wind down.

Scampering past the three cowering victims of the bird's attack, K.C. headed homewards, duty done for the day. He congratulated himself on the completion of a very successful mission, under what he would have described as extremely difficult conditions. Perhaps now he would be able to regain his rightful place as commander and, he puffed his chest out, could even put himself up for an award. A bravery medal would be nice. Grinning triumphantly, he poked his head through the hole in the hedgerow. It was good to be back among friends.

153

Chapter 16

Digger had had just about enough. Whoever came through that hole was in for a damn good thump! C'mon, he thought, hurry…

Quicker than he had anticipated, emerging from the hedge and coming directly towards him was a large blurry shape, and what seemed to be just what he was waiting for. The perfect target. He almost allowed the figure to escape, because, somewhere at the back of his mind was something Albert had said he should not do, or was it something he should? Whatever, or whoever, the hell it was, it was too late now, and, anyway, he had waited long enough. Closing his claws into a fist, he timed the punch perfectly, catching the unsuspecting target flush on the jaw. Knocking not only the tortoise shell from the spaniel's mouth but loosening several of K.C.'s front teeth.

Albert couldn't believe what he had just witnessed. "Why the hell did you do that? You flattened the dog!"

"Dog? What dog?" Digger looked across at the spaniel, who was just regaining his feet. "Oh, that dog. Sorry."

Then he remembered that he didn't do apologies and blamed K.C. "It was your own fault!" he admonished the spaniel. "You should have called out." Adding insult to K.C.'s injury, he added, "I can't see what all the fuss is about! It was only a gentle tap." The dog was a wuss anyway.

"You thug!" K.C. complained, "How am I thuppoted to thouth with a mouth full of tortoith thell?"

Albert and Digger looked at the expression on K.C.'s face and burst out laughing.

"Barth, Barth," the spaniel tried ordering the pair to stop their laughter. "Thop ith! Ith's not funny!" He expected nothing less from those two peasants, so he turned to plead with Speedy for a little sympathy. The tortoise was nowhere to be seen. "Anyone theen Thpeedy?"

"Who the hell is Thpeedy?" they both wanted to know.

"Thpeedy," K.C. barked in frustration. "Thpeedy, the tortoith. You damn ignoramuths!"

Albert eventually understood K.C.'s lisp. "Oh, Speedy. No, I haven't. Not since the bird attack."

Very concerned for their missing friend, the three of them began a search of the area. Albert and Digger, both grinning insanely, calling out, "Thpeedy, Thpeedy?"

He was nowhere to be seen; even Albert's sensitive tongue had been unable to detect him. He voiced what the other two had probably been thinking: that his best mate was no more. "One of the birds must have taken him by mistake. He must have looked very appetising to one of them."

After searching for a second time, they all had to agree Speedy was gone.

"Might ath well go," K.C. suggested, "before Billy and his minders recover and dethide to come looking for uth."

Amazing! Albert reflected, when the hound didn't have a lisp, I couldn't understand a word he was saying. Now he's speaking with a lisp, I understand him perfectly. Weird. "Yeah, I suppose you are right. C'mon, let's get going."

Digger, unsurprisingly, wanted to inflict more pain. "Why don't we stay and have a bundle anyway?"

Still in a bit of a fug, his mouth yet to start hurting, and for the moment forgetting it was the mole who was responsible for his front teeth being loose, K.C. put a consoling paw across Digger's shoulder. "We tried our best, old boy. We tried." Suddenly, realising the danger he was in, he leapt backwards, scampering to safety behind Albert.

With heavy hearts, the trio turned to go.

"Oi, you lot! Wait for me!"

It was the missing tortoise.

Delighted to see his friend, Albert hissed, "Where the hell have you been?" Even more of a shock, Speedy had his shell back on. "And where did you get the shell from?"

"It's mine," Speedy huffed. Where did he think I got it from? Shells 4 U?

"I know it's yours, you muffin! I meant, how did you get it back? The last I saw of it the bloody thing was sailing back over the hedge!"

Speedy explained. When the birds began to attack everyone on this side of the hedgerow, he decided it was safer to hide under the bushes. "I saw the bombers arrive, so decided to stay where I was. After the second attack began on Billy, I was about to come back when I was almost flattened by the flying shell." He went on. "The reason I am late? I struggled to get back into the shell. Then I sprinted back as quickly as I could, to see you all legging it. Thank you very much!"

Albert's interpretation of speed and Speedy's differed somewhat, but now wasn't the time or the place to go into it. The birds had called off their attack on Billy and his mates. It was time to go.

The insane birds had at last tired and flown back into the trees. Two, though, had been stunned when Billy's hooves caught the pair a glancing blow. Unable to escape, the birds, a starling and a rook, were swiftly and viciously dispatched by the two dogs, Knuckles and Nipper.

Getting over the shock of the unwarranted assault, Billy was hell-bent on revenge. Someone had put the birds up to the attack, and whoever it had been was going to pay, and pay dearly. That albino dog – the one who had taken his shell – would do for starters. And Knuckles had a grievance and would quickly sort out the coward who had broken his nose. He knew that whoever had directed the birds to attack them hadn't gone far, because he could still hear their voices. And was that laughter? Were they making fun of him? Well, he would soon give them something to chuckle about. No one laughs at Billy the Hat and gets away with it.

On Albert's side of the hedge, he ordered Speedy on to the frisbee, directing K.C.to begin pulling, get to the bridge and get across as quickly as possible.

Billy, meanwhile, had been trying to push aside enough of the hedgerow to squeeze his head through. At first, he had expected to see the white-washed spaniel and possibly the one responsible for Knuckles' injured snout. What he most certainly wasn't expecting was to be confronted by a smelly odd-coloured adder, but nonetheless, a living breathing adder who, it seemed to him, was about to take a bite-sized chunk off his nose. Backing away pretty smartish, he unfortunately reversed into the advancing Knuckles, accidentally stamping on the bulldog's nose, making it bleed once more.

Already on a bit of a low, Knuckles retaliated, biting Billy hard on the ankle. Instinctively, the ram kicked out, inflicting even more pain on Knuckles, sending the wounded canine sprawling, and complaining, "You bit me!"

"Well, you should be more careful where you tread!"

The bulldog groaned, wiping his sore and bleeding nose on the grass.

The Jack Russell terrier, having seen his mate come back from the hedge with his nose bleeding, and then having watched his boss reversing as if he was being chased by a posse of butchers, asked if there was anything he could to help? Billy explained what was going on, telling Nipper, "Yeah, go through the hedge, have a look and report back. It's safe enough now."

The Jack Russell cautiously slipped through the greenery. Seeing no one, he barked the all-clear. "Okay, Boss. No one's here."

"You sure, Nipper?"

Warily, Billy followed, poking his head through the hedge. The terrier was right. Everyone had gone. Pushing and shoving, the ram made a big enough hole for himself and Knuckles to squeeze through.

"Which way did they go?" Billy asked the normally reliable bulldog.

Knuckles growled, "Dow am I thupposed to dho? My dose ith broken."

It was Nipper who picked up the scent. "They went that way, Boss, towards the old bridge, and by their scent, they haven't gone far."

"Okay. Nipper, as you are uninjured, you take the lead. Knuckles, you go second, and I'll watch your backs. Right. We know that there are at least two of them. Let's go and sort them out!"

Billy considered it a good idea to let the others go first, having been only six inches away from the business end of a poisonous adder. And he thought it best not to tell his friends they were also chasing a very poisonous snake. If he had, he didn't think they would have been so keen to have taken the lead.

*   *   *

For the third time in as many yards, Speedy tumbled out of his frisbee. Towing the sled at walking pace and without his shell had been fine. Now at speed and fully dressed, it had become impossible for him to get a grip on the sides of the plastic carriage.

Earlier, Albert had sent the protesting mole on his way, but not before he had almost got the obligatory mouthful of mole fur. Making the mistake of telling Digger, firstly, to keep both eyes peeled, then compounding his slip by reminding him to keep in close eye contact with the two of them, it had been a near thing. He watched Digger zigzag after K.C. and Speedy. Now he was ready to put the final part of his plan into place. He had been reluctant to put this part of it into force, for everyone's sake, enemy as well as friends, but just in case. A minute later, he caught up with his friends. It was explained to him by K.C. the difficulty Speedy was having keeping a tight grip to the edges of the frisbee. With the tortoise unable to hold on and slowing them down, it looked like now he had no choice. It was the only way out. Incredulously he ordered Speedy to tell him a joke.

"What?" Speedy almost choked. The snake had obviously lost the plot. "Tell you a joke? Have you gone barmy, or what?"

Albert was insistent. "Tell me a joke and make me laugh."

"I...I can't remember any." Only the one, he thought, where, by the time I have got to the punchline, we all get savaged. "Honest, Albert."

K.C. eventually managed to get his voice back. "Thnake, can we thtop playing thilly gameth and go now, pleath?" he lisped, as desperate as Speedy to be off.

Not so Digger. A delay of any kind brought him closer to having the bundle he had been desperately waiting for. "Tell the silly sod a joke! And be quick about it!"

Then, with a little help from Albert, he waddled back down the path to guard the rear. Needless to say, Albert omitted to mention anything about keeping an eye out.

Speedy was in a bit of a quandary. What would be worse? Beaten up by a psycho who was less than a foot from him, or tell a joke no one in their right mind would laugh at, or wait and be ready to be savaged? Well, he hoped, Albert knew what he was doing. Clearing his dry throat, he began what could be the last joke of his life. Perhaps he and his friends were about to die laughing.

"B...bloke walking through the park sees a chap sat next to a huge gorilla and asks if his gorilla is safe. The chap on the bench says, 'Of course, my gorilla is safe'. Satisfied, the first bloke then pats the animal on the head. With that, the gorilla jumps up and almost rips the bloke to bits, leaving him bruised and bloodied. Satisfied, the gorilla then sits back down. Stunned and in shock, the injured man looks at the fellow on the bench and says, 'I thought you said your gorilla was safe?' Chap gets up from the bench, walks away and says, 'That's not my gorilla'."

Nothing. Not a giggle, a titter, smirk or even a half-smile from any of them. Speedy gave Albert a 'You berk', look and ducked into his shell

Had he just made the biggest and last mistake of his life? To reinforce his fears, he could hear the chasing pack fast approaching. It wouldn't be long now before they were on them.

Suddenly, from the long grass came a chuckle and then a full-throated belly laugh, followed immediately by reverberating wind echoing throughout the meadow.

"Rrripppp."

Pongo! The fart noises were only a foretaste; the curtain-raiser of what was to come. The stench would quickly follow.

The foul air was fast approaching the chasers, beginning to fill the whole area. There would be nowhere for them to hide. No escape. And to help his friends, Pongo had devoured an extra helping of bog weed and slime; ensuring that the stink would be fouler and deadlier than his earlier assault.

The chasing trio's sensory organs were about to be assaulted as never before. Pongo was about to do his friends proud. He only hoped they would come to appreciate the effort he was putting in for them.

"Run," Albert warned, "before it's too late!"

He was alone. His friends had already deserted him. Charming! he thought, slithering quickly after them.

K.C. had been the first away. He had heard that laughter earlier in the day and knew exactly what was to come next. He winced as he picked up Speedy from the stationary frisbee. Sore jaw or not, physical pain was a damn sight more bearable than having to breathe in the frog's farts. One small whiff of frog innards would suffice for today.

Digger, however, was going nowhere. Never having run away from a fight – or anything else for that matter – he was determined he wasn't going to start now. He readied himself for the longed-for upcoming to-do. A shift in the breeze and he instantly changed his mind; his blurry vision for the moment no longer a handicap. He took off after K.C., leaving Albert to get on with it. It was, after all, the snake's daft idea in the first place.

All the time slowing down and falling further behind, Albert had begun to tire, his energy levels now dangerously low. Usually at this time of year, like most adders, he spent a lot of his time basking in the sun, so it was no surprise he was starting to flag just a little. Less than ten yards behind him, closing fast, Nipper.

Suddenly, the terrier stopped dead in his tracks, his eyes watering and screwing up, shut tight. What the hell is that smell? His nose, the most sensitive now that Nipper was unable to breathe through his, was the first to notice the stench. His paws scratched insanely at his tortured snout, unable to believe that anything could smell so rotten. Whatever it was, it must have died years ago. Perhaps chasing his tail would help? No, of course it wouldn't, but it didn't stop him from at least trying.

In fact, the stench seemed to stick to his tongue. Out of breath, he stopped to take a breather. Gulping in what he assumed would be fresh air, he inhaled more of the foul unclean atmosphere. Down he went. What had been stuck up his ruined nasal organ had now moved to his internal organs and was savaging his lungs, almost causing him to eject his lunch. What had he ever done to deserve such torment? Legs twitching, he looked across at the seemingly unaffected bulldog. It must have been him, the dirty sod! What the hell had he been eating? Eyes pleading for the torture to stop, and whimpering insanely, he collapsed once again. This time the stench did for him. His final thought before blacking out was how to get his own back on that dirty sod Knuckles.

Next to feel the effects of recycled frog farts was Billy; all thoughts of retribution soon to be gone. He was about to ask Nipper why he was playing silly buggers when he got his first whiff of the foul odour. Bleating insanely and, just like Nipper, he began running around in circles, his effort to escape the foul odour a futile waste of time. Whichever direction he ran in, the stench doggedly followed. Living on a sheep farm, he had had his share of foul smells to cope with. But this! He could even taste it. "Baa, baaing" desperately, as a last resort he head-butted one of the trees. That didn't help either, except to give him a headache. His nasal organ eventually mutinied and refused to take any more punishment, and down he went to join Nipper writhing about on the floor. Why, oh why, hadn't the farmer decided to have roast lamb for his Sunday lunch?

Unlike Billy and company, Pongo, from his grandstand view in the grass, continued to fart with gay abandon. He was loving it. Laughing so much, his throat was getting husky; even his bum was getting a bit hoarse. Eventually he just couldn't emit any more of the foul wind. Job done, he decided to return to the pond.

He was very lucky he had run out of ammunition when he did. He didn't know it but, as it had turned out, it was at an opportune and lifesaving moment. Knuckles had heard the frog laughing and farting and had, eventually, worked out what was going on and had found Pongo's location. He was about to pounce when the frog ran out of wind and disappeared into the undergrowth. Unable, because of his bloody nose, to sniff out the location of the reeking amphibian, Knuckles returned to his prostrate friends.

Meanwhile, now back at the pond, Pongo waited. He was very much looking forward to greeting his friends later. Perhaps, after all the hard work he had put in to help them, they would, next time, welcome him with big smiles and not the usual tortured grimaces.

Knuckles was in a bit of a dilemma. Should he stay and help his wounded comrades or carry on alone? After all, he had plenty of unfinished business to attend to. Explaining the situation to his tortured and twitching companions, neither of whom cared one jot what the heck he did next anyway, he headed for the old bridge. Whoever it was he caught up with first, they would be on the receiving end of one hell of a good hiding, and whoever it was would remember the meeting for a very long time afterwards. If indeed, for them, there was an afterwards.

Chapter 17

With Speedy clamped firmly in his sore mouth, K.C. was first to cross the rickety bridge. Ominously, the wooden structure began to groan and sag beneath him, almost causing him to yelp and drop the tortoise; the spaniel and Speedy's combined weight almost too much for the rotten timbers.

Digger, puffing and panting, unused to this much exercise above ground, waited until the pair in front had cleared the bridge before he attempted to get across. He too felt the structure move. Joining K.C. and Speedy, they waited for Albert.

On the bridge, exhausted and seemingly unable to drag himself the few remaining yards to safety, Albert turned to face his pursuer: the bloody-nosed bulldog. He would have to defend himself for real this time.

It was already too late. Taking a massive leap, Knuckles was on him, removing what little oxygen Albert had left in his lungs. It mattered little to the bulldog who or what he had been pursuing. Whether it was the swine who had earlier broken his nose or this dung-covered snake, he would take his revenge. Powerful paws held Albert's head to the rotten timbers. There was nothing Albert could do. For a second time today, he awaited the inevitable.

His friends looked on in horror as the canine prepared to finish the snake off. Digger would have gone to help his friend if he could have seen straight to get on to the bridge.

Suddenly, the structure lurched dangerously, dropping by almost a foot. The bulldog, unsure what was happening, momentarily released his grip. This was Albert's chance to escape. Sliding forward, he managed to manoeuvre himself a few precious feet away from Knuckles, almost making it to safety.

Ceasing its dangerous motion almost immediately, the bridge became still once more; its creaking timbers the only reminder of what had just happened.

The angry canine had a decision to make. Get off the bridge and go back, or finish what he had promised himself and his mates he was going to do: give someone a damn good hiding. It was no contest. Now, where the hell had the snake got to?

Albert was less than a foot from solid ground when the canine leapt for a second time, again landing squarely on the back of his exposed neck. This time, the bridge had had enough; the weight of the dog crashing down for a second time too much for the ageing timber. Fate, once again, albeit temporarily, had intervened on Albert's behalf. Snake, canine and the fragile bridge collapsed into the river below, everything sinking beneath the murky waters.

First to reappear was Knuckles. Coughing and spluttering, he paddled his way to the safety of the far riverbank, opposite to where Albert's stunned friends had watched the drama unfold. Then, piece by rotten piece, the remnants of the destroyed walkway returned to the surface, each broken section floating gently downstream.

Of Albert, there was no sign.

First to recover was K.C. "Mmpph, Mmpph," he barked, for a moment forgetting he had a mouthful of tortoise shell. Unceremoniously, he spat out Speedy; the ejected tortoise landing head-first in the soil.

Spluttering and coughing, Speedy complained, "Oi! What did you do that for? My mouth is full of grit now!"

Digger was his usual self. "That's because your brains are leaking. Now shut it, or else!" He looked at K.C. "All right then, you, what next?"

"Mole," K.C. directed, "you look upthream, and I'll try downthream. Tortoith, you thtay put. And if Albert cometh back, thout for uth. Got it?"

And with that, he was gone.

Speedy frowned. "What did he say, Digger? I didn't understand a word of it, and why is he talking like that?"

The mole didn't have the time to go into explanations right now, so, instead, warned, "Come here and I'll show you why." Before he could follow up on his threat, he heard K.C. barthing. He should help, and go and look for Albert. Blinking and winking, his vision again back to being one-sided, he carefully made his way to the water's edge. "Oi, snake!" he called. "Stop buggering about and get your backside back here! Or else!" (If he knew what was good for him.) As he had expected, there was no reply. He waddled back to where Speedy waited.

"Any luck?" Speedy was desperate to hear some good news.

"Yeah. I've got him tucked under my arm."

Seeing how disappointed Speedy was, he relented a little. "Sorry."

Meanwhile, K.C. had gone about fifty yards downriver, barth, barthing Albert's name, sadly with the same result as Digger. Disconsolately, he made his way back to his two friends with the sad news. Nothing. For the first time today, all were in total agreement. It was likely they would never see their friend again. He was dead.

*   *   *

Albert wasn't dead; he was very much alive! For the time being at least, he was just about clinging on to life. Although he was wishing he wasn't clinging on to anything. Able to wrap his tail around a section of broken handrail, it had helped him float to the surface, although much further downstream than K.C. had anticipated.

What had originally saved him from drowning now, perversely, threatened to finish him off. The rotten piece of handrail had become wedged underwater a tantalising six inches from the riverbank. Unluckily for Albert, his tail was still firmly trapped by the submerged piece of flotsam. In his exhaustion, he was unable to free himself and realised his only hope now would be his friends, if they thought to look this far from the bridge. Despite wasting precious breath, he called out. No reply.

Desperate now, he went under for perhaps the third time. Once again, he managed – just – to raise his head above the cold water. It was getting harder to stay on the surface, to keep his head above water. He thought about Granny Anna and her philosophy for staying safe. "If believing never stops," she had reminded him, "you never stop believing."

Giving it one final effort, he stretched his already overextended scales. It was no good. He was still stuck. Sorry Granny Anna, but I did try. He began to slip under for the final time.

"Thnake! Thnake! Barth, barth! Don't you drown, you damnable reptile!"

Now Albert was starting to hallucinate, to hear voices.

"Barth, barth!"

He at last recognised K.C.'s barking lisp. "K.C.!" Albert called desperately, "I'm over here!"

The spaniel, again – as always – not content to urinate were he stood, had left the others in order to search for a suitable target to pee on and had sniffed his way downstream. While he was delighted that Albert that was still alive, although he looked like he was in serious trouble, he nevertheless realised that this was an opportunity that was too good to miss. Cocking his leg, he took careful aim, urinated and hit his target squarely on the nose. Bullseye! He congratulated himself. Got the bounder at last!

Albert, coughing and spluttering, his mouth already full of mud and dirty water, now had the indignity of getting a mouthful of dog pee.

Obviously, K.C. had yet to seen him.

"Oi, I'm here! My tail is trapped and it's too dificu…"

This time he swallowed the squirt of warm wee. "Will you stop doing that!" he spluttered. "My tail's coming loose, but I haven't got the strength to pull anymore."

His bladder now well and truly empty, a very satisfied K.C. sat down and began scratching behind an ear. He was thinking.

"Well?" Albert managed. "Are you to going to help me, or what?"

K.C. suggested that Albert 'thut' his mouth.

"WHAT?" He was dumbstruck, "Don't tell me to thut – shut – my mouth! I'm the one who's drowning, or hadn't you noticed?"

K.C. explained what he had in mind and Albert had the good sense to do as he was told to do and kept his mouth firmly shut.

"NOW!" the spaniel barthed.

Opening his jaws wide, K.C. made a grab for Albert's head. At the same time, Albert thrust his body as far forward as it would go as if he was about to bite K.C. in self-defence. Catching the snake at his first attempt, the spaniel bit down hard. The first two inches of Albert disappeared into his mouth. Albert was too exhausted to care whether or not the dog took his head off. Luckily, thanks to a half-blind mole's violence,

K.C.'s front teeth weren't fully aligned, so, happily, Albert's head remained where it had always been.

Pulling and tugging, K.C. eventually managed to dislodge the weary snake from the unwanted anchor, hauling him up the bank to safety before finally disgorging his grateful passenger.

But something was wrong. Albert was safe, but now his friend seemed to be struggling. Tongue lolling out of his mouth, coughing hoarsely, paw scratching at his tongue, the poor chap seemed to be choking. Was he attempting to remove something that had lodged at the back of his throat? Had the spaniel inadvertently swallowed mud from the stream? Albert was beginning to feel more than a little concerned.

He needn't have worried. K.C. was only admonishing himself. How could he have been so utterly stupid, so utterly irresponsible? Suppose the damn snake's teeth had leaked? And what would have happened if he had been bitten? He was feeling decidedly sick. Never, ever again, he swore to himself. The next time the damn snake could drown.

Having got his breath back, Albert slithered over to enquire if the spaniel needed his assistance. Perhaps he could help locate the blockage, assist in cleaning out any pieces of mud from his throat? K.C., eyes wide, gave Albert a withering look, yelped and scrambled quickly away.

Funny bugger, Albert decided.

Digger and Speedy arrived just in time to see the spaniel scampering away; both surprised but delighted to see their friend alive. Albert explained how K.C had saved his life, sensibly omitting the part where he had been peed on. Knowing the ribbing he would have taken, perhaps that was for the best.

Digger enquired, "Where's he off to now?"

"Why?" Albert enquired. "What's up?"

"Well, I was thinking of lamping him one again. But then again, it wouldn't seem fair now, would it?"

Albert considered it for a moment, agreeing with Digger. No, it wouldn't be right.

Digger thought about it for a second, winked at Albert; this time though a genuine flicker. "Hey, 'Poshterior'!" he called to the fast retreating spaniel. "Come here, you! We've still got some unfinished business to sort out."

Hotly pursued by the one-eyed mole, the dog with wobbly front teeth barthed his defiance and made his getaway.

Speedy giggled happily, glad the mole had picked on someone who could run away. He was glad also that, thanks to his friends, he wasn't homeless anymore.

Albert laughed as the mole slammed head-first into one of his own redundant molehills. He had obviously winked when he should have blinked.

With a happy sigh, Albert looked around the meadow. Everything seemed to be returning to normal again. Or, as normal as it would ever get in this strange place.

THE END

©©©

Lightning Source UK Ltd.
Milton Keynes UK
UKHW020712090820
367908UK00011B/704